Behind The Red Curtain

BEHIND
THE RED
CURTAIN

Casey Bartsch

For Lucy.
Because, even though she is basically the worst friend ever, she will always have a very special place in my heart.

PART 1
CATCH

CHAPTER 1

"I'm sorry, but we no longer carry Tutti-Frutti."

"Why the fuck not?" the overtly disgruntled man said.

"Because, sir, we rotate our flavors on a monthly basis. We find that our customers enjoy the change."

"Well not me! Am I not a customer? It is inexcusable that..." *Etc*.

Lucinda could ignore the rest of the conversation, as she had heard it all before. Customers always complained about the flavor changes, and she had already brought it up with the owner several times. His interest was non-existent, being too busy scouring the earth for bugs that he could name after himself. He was an entomologist who just happened to own a gourmet popcorn shop. In fact, he owned the entire strip mall in which *Poppin' Fresh* resided.

Her preferred method of revenge for unruly customers was calculated apathy, as they hated when she wasn't affected by their ravings. The customer simply couldn't be right all the time, and sometimes Lucy needed a win in her own column.

"We will have that flavor again in a few months. In the meantime, can I offer you our newest flavor – s'mores?"

"I don't want fucking s'mor...
Etc.

The shop was small, and Lucy only managed two other employees; both as worthless as a vibrator without batteries. Sure, they do the job – but not very well. The male of the two, Tommy, had called in sick. This was commonplace and based on his girlfriend's sexual availability. The female, Cassidy, was present and accounted-for but was predictably hunched over in a corner doing homework. She liked to speak math problems out loud, a habit that Lucy had yet to get used to. At forty-two, Lucy was older than the both of them combined, and she was happy to pretend that she wasn't at all bothered by that fact. But, it was what it was, and nothing else. When it came right down to it, her job was not a taxing one, help or no help.

Usually.

When the annoying little bell on the front door twinkled its evil sound, and she was forced to stop her paperwork to take care of the front counter so that Cassidy could continue her education, she was dismayed at what was waiting for her there.

The kids had come into the shop twice before, and it hadn't gone well either time. They wore stereotypical black– ripped jeans and bad attitudes. Hooligans all, Lucy's mother would have said. She stayed silent, having learned that the sound of her voice only exacerbated things. Their leader, a slim slime ball of an adolescent, sauntered over to the counter as the other two boys fanned out.

"Hey, hey!" the slime ball said, "Look who it is, guys. The same lady that was so very nice to us the last time we were here."

"Can I help you, *sir*?"

"Sure, you can. We just stopped in for a bite to eat. Go ahead and eat up," he said, motioning to the walls lined with popcorn bags. The other two boys immediately began to rip down bags and bust them open, occasionally taking a bite, but mostly scattering the kernels across the floor, and it wasn't long before everything was covered in a rainbow of tasty treats. Lucy wasn't bothered. A little sweeping was better than letting these guys ruin her night.

She had read *The Power of Positive Thinking* from cover to cover. Twice.

Cassidy, hearing the commotion, called out, "Is everything cool up there?"

"Yeah, Cass, just do your homework," she answered.

Their fearless leader looked over Lucy's shoulder to see where the voice had come from. When he saw Cassidy, he smiled and licked his lips in a way that Lucinda had seen far too many times in her life. She hated the perversion that resided in his eyes, and she could no longer play the placid counter girl role.

"Why don't you idiot kids get out of here? You've got nothing better to do with your time than spill popcorn on the floor?"

"You shut your damn face lady! We do what we want, and today we are hungry for popcorn," he said, pulling a pocket knife from his pants pocket. There was so much shit stuffed in his pants that it was comic gold watching him dig the thing out. Still, the sudden addition of a blade into the mix didn't ease her mind.

"Well, may I suggest our newest flavor – s'mores. It's just 2.99 for a small bag; 4.99 for a large."

"Shut up, bitch!" the boy said, swiftly reaching out and grabbing Lucy by her shirt collar. He raised the knife up near her face, and she was just about to pull away when the brass bell rang – the sound decidedly less annoying this time than usual. A man, dressed in the nicest suit that Lucy had ever seen, took a single step inside and stood in front of the door.

Authority dripped from the man's skin, and power was his fragrance. All three boys stopped and looked at him, and the slime ball released her collar. A few moments of silence later, one of them politely asked, "The fuck do you want?"

"To get some popcorn, of course. I am in the right place, aren't I?" he asked, smooth as silk.

"Now isn't the time, fella. Fuck off," said the slime ball.

"That language isn't really appropriate while a lady is present, and it seems to me that you gentlemen have made quite the mess," the man said, looking down at the floor. "I believe that the three of you should 'fuck off' instead."

The boys summoned whatever underlying machismo that puberty had cursed them with, puffed their chests, and stood their ground. The dapper man took a step to the side and motioned to the door, unfazed by the territorial display. Something in his face caused the boys to think again. Lucy could see it too.

The man was stone.

None of the boys wanted to be the first to back down, afraid to be the pussy of the group. But, the man was unwavering, and their resolve was not. All three moved toward the door together. Slimeball made one more gallant attempt to save his masculinity by abruptly motioning to the man's face as he passed, trying to make him flinch. He didn't get his wish, and as he exited the popcorn shop, the words, "Man, fuck off," could be heard, ever so faintly.

Acting as if nothing at all had happened, the man walked over to the right wall and browsed what was left. As he walked, he brushed aside the popcorn with his fancy clad feet. He looked at the wall for quite some time. Lucy had been planning to thank him when he came to the register, but he was taking so long, that she was beginning to feel like a real jerk for not saying anything already.

She quickly said, "Thank you," fully realizing that she sounded like an oafish child.

Without turning to her, he said, "Oh, no problem. Kids can be a bit ridiculous when there isn't someone in their lives to keep them in line and offer perspective."

He reached up and grabbed a bag of white cheddar and another of plain caramel, then looked up at a list of flavors written on a chalkboard hung on the wall.

"No Tutti-Frutti this month?"

"No, I'm sorry. We rotate them out."

"Makes sense. Don't want to keep things too predictable and bland. I'll just take these two." He removed a wallet from the inside pocket of his suit jacket as he approached the counter, still deftly removing any popcorn from his stride. He placed the bags down and asked, "How much do I owe you?"

"Oh, those are on the house. Thanks so much, again."

He smiled at her appreciatively, but said, "I wouldn't dream of letting you do that. It was my pleasure, really. And, my mother always said, 'Good deeds need no reward.'"

"Are you sure?"

"Positive."

"Well then," Lucy said, punching the numbers into the register, "That's 10.78 with tax."

As he handed her a twenty, he looked up and smiled; his eyes tethered to her own. "You know, if I could manage to go against my mother's wishes and accept thanks, perhaps you would like to show your gratitude by letting me take you out for coffee?"

The proposition caught Lucy off guard. She felt like the captain of the football team had just asked her to prom instead of the head cheerleader. Would she have pig blood on her head at the end of the date, because this man was clearly one of means and measure? One look at his clothes, BMW parked outside, and perfectly straight, white teeth could show anyone that he was out of her league.

That smile.

Why would he consider me a valid option, even on his worst day?

"Well, yes. Okay. I can do that," she said, having no other option.

When life throws you flowers, you don't say "No thank you, I'll wait for the dirt."

"That's fantastic," he said, "You've made my day. Popcorn and a date all at once. Actually, I was just thinking – would you like to go to the theater with me? Do you enjoy a play?"

"That sounds nice, but I will be honest and tell you that I haven't been to many."

"Even better. It will be even more special. How is tomorrow night?"

"I work 'til eight."

"Not a problem. I will pick you up right here. Sound good?"

Fuck yes it does.

"Sounds fine. See you then."

He spun around to leave, but his eyes trailed behind, as if he were trying to get as much of a look at Lucy as he could. The night had become unreal. Her legs were like rubber, and she didn't even hear the infernal bell ring as he left.

How could this have happened to her?

"Everything ok up there?"

"Yeah Cassidy, just – seriously, do your homework."

Cassidy had packed her books and headed home over an hour ago– not that she would have been a giant help closing the store anyway. The girl meant well, but she was more adept at stumbling into Lucy's way than she was at anything else. Besides, this was actually Lucy's favorite part of the job. She was alone in the store, the lights were turned down low, and the sign was flipped to "closed." She turned up her music – an eclectic mix of all the genres grandparents hated – and she breathed deep. Even the rancid smell of 20 flavors of popcorn couldn't ruin the relaxation of an empty store.

Who was that man?

Lucy hadn't even gotten his name, and he hadn't asked for hers either.

You wear a nametag, you dolt.

Still, she couldn't fathom it. Why would he ask her out? She wasn't exactly a spring chicken, and what she did have to offer visually wasn't anything special. Looking down at her shabby work clothes, tarnished with crusty bits and mystery stains, she felt embarrassed. She certainly wasn't altogether unattractive, but in this uniform, she may as well be a hobo clown riding the rails.

In contrast, the man seemed so otherworldly. He had an air about him that was beyond her comprehension. It wasn't just the expensive car and clothes, but more the way he presented *himself*. He was regal without a crown, a knight without a sword.

A picture that escaped the frame.

She was getting nervous. Thinking about their impending date was making her heart speed up, and her vision slow down. At that moment, she wished to hell that they had exchanged numbers. She would text him right then and cancel–just make some shit up.

Her mom died.

Her mom was dying.

Her mom may very well be working for a covert organization, and now Lucy's own life has been put in danger. She must leave the confines of the popcorn shop and dash to parts unknown. If he was questioned, she begged him not tell a soul that he had crossed paths with her.

But, she didn't have his number, and he would be there tomorrow to pick her up. She made a quick reminder on her cell phone to bring a change of clothes, then she sat down on some boxes in the corner and sighed. Her brain needed to catch its breath, and she decided that the floor would not get mopped tonight.

"The worst thing that could possibly happen is that he just won't like you," she said out loud to the wall. "That leaves you no worse off than you are now."

Positive Thinking – everyone should read it.

She was right. It would be nothing. He probably had some deep-seated complex that made him desire women that he deemed unfortunate, or perhaps he just felt an obligation for saving her. She continued to tell herself things like that, trying to play the man down in her mind, but always there was a tiny thought stuck in the back of her brain. That teensy nagging spark that told her that he may like her, and she may like him back.

Happily ever after.

Lucy had no reason to believe that she could still hope for such a fairy tale. It hadn't worked out the last couple of times. Maybe that was it for her. Perhaps she was relegated to the spinster life, settling for an occasional, unsatisfying lay from desperate men at the bar down the street. She had never been in the joint, but it was always an option.

Lucy looked the shop over, and though it was a complete fib, she judged it clean. She counted the till and stashed the cash in the floor safe. Taking out the garbage was the only remaining task before she could go home to her bathtub to sink in and daydream. Maybe she would light candles and have some wine, though she would have to stop and get some. She had polished off her last bottle two nights ago. Maybe, instead of dreaming of better things, she could read a book, and get lost in someone else's vision of "better things."

She grabbed the two heaping bags of trash she had stashed by the back door and used her back to push out into the night air. The sweet scent of garbage juice filled her nostrils to the point that she tasted it on her tongue, and it oozed from her ears. Lucy didn't bother to walk all the way to the trash bin, choosing instead to throw the bags in the general direction of the dumpster.

The first bag fell into the bin with a satisfying crackle, but the second slipped from her fingers too early and crashed into the side. Stale popcorn exploded out on the ground, and she immediately knew that there was no way she would clean it up. She would have an underling clear it tomorrow – if the rodents and birds didn't take care of it themselves.

Rushing away from the smell, Lucy pulled her keys from her cluttered excuse for a purse. Like every night, she began to get a little shiver in her spine. Empty, dark parking lots were never her best friend.

As she rounded the corner of the building, she at once saw that her car was not the only one in the lot as usual. The BMW from before was parked alongside her aging Toyota. Her heart fluttered in her chest as fear gripped its wings.

There was no reason for him to be here.

Maybe he couldn't wait to see you.

She didn't know which thought to listen to. She stopped in her tracks and contemplated whether to go back inside the shop, or move toward her car. She could wait him out in the shop. She wouldn't die in the shop. She could breathe in there, and come up with a plan.

But, *he* was over there. The man that bucked the odds and asked her out. If she turned away from him now, maybe he would come to his senses and realize that she wasn't worth the hassle.

Before she could decide, the door to the Beamer opened and the man stepped out. It was dark, but she could still see the smile on his face. She became acutely aware of how long she had been standing there, dumbstruck, with keys held out in front of her.

"I hope you don't mind," he called out, "But, I was hoping that maybe you would like to have that date tonight."

She stood speechless still unsure. Was this a blessing or a danger? Her gut told her to go back inside, but every other part of her wanted to call out to the man and gladly accept.

Her gut lost miserably, and it wasn't even a real contest.

As she timidly walked forward, the man came around his car and leaned against the passenger side. He was wearing an entirely different suit than he had on before, and Lucy admired his attire as she remembered her own again.

Crusty bits.

Shit, I am disgusting.

"I don't think I am in any shape for going out," she said, and meant it.

"Are you worried about a dress code?" he asked.

"I'm worried about the smell. Code or not, I would like to change first. Is that okay? I don't live far. I could take a quick shower and meet you - wherever."

"I think you look splendid. I like a woman after she has worked. There is a glow of accomplishment about you."

"I think that glow may just be the fumes from the dumpster back there."

He laughed at the joke, disarming her instantly.

"How about I follow you back to your place? I'll wait patiently in my car, like a perfect gentleman. Then, we can go and have a wonderful first date."

Her gut again. It was relentless.

"That should be okay. I think," she said. "But, I'd hate to make you just wait in your car. Are you sure you don't just want me to meet you?"

"Absolutely," the man said, as he walked to the driver's side of Lucy's car. He rested his hand on the handle and smiled as she clicked the button to unlock the door, then he opened it wide and bowed ever so slightly. He was laying on the chivalry thick, which normally would have made Lucy balk. In this case, it made her swoon. She wasn't sure at that moment if she had ever swooned in her entire life.

When she was about to step into her car, he placed his hand on the small of her back, and her previous shivers of fear were replaced with tingles of a different sort. She couldn't wait to get home and change so this man could touch her again, which is why she felt confusion at the sharp pain in her neck.

The needle felt like a hornet sting and immediately caused her vision to blur. It was only a moment later that her legs became a soft mush and could no longer hold her. Lucy's final thought, as the man's arms caught her under the shoulders and began to drag her away, was that she should have listened to her gut.

At least he didn't let her hit the pavement.

Then, darkness took her.

CHAPTER 2

Her father's silhouette was as big as the world with the sun shining like a glorious beacon. Lucy raised her hand and traced his outline, trying hard to ignore the pain in her knee. The dirt beneath her was warm to the touch, the rocks hot enough to sting her skin.

"What happened?" her father asked.

"I wasn't looking where I was going."

"That's right. Own your mistake. That's very good."

Lucy lifted her body up and saw the blood trailing down her leg, bits of gravel embedded in her flesh.

"Does it hurt?"

"Yes."

"Wrong. Pain is not something you feel. It is a momentary lapse in reason. You take that pain and mold it like clay until it becomes a memory. One that you can always look back on and remember. This is how we don't repeat our mistakes."

"Yes, Daddy."

She got back to her feet and brushed herself off as best she could. They still had several miles left to hike, and if they were to get there before the sun set, she would have to hurry. Her knee throbbed, but Lucy began to mold it.

She wasn't going to let a cut up leg ruin her eighth birthday.

The pain in Lucy's head was unrepentantly aggressive as she attempted to open her eyelids. They would not immediately co-operate, and as she attempted to raise a hand to her face, she realized that she could not move. Through sheer will she managed to crack open her eyes and slowly tried to blink the world into focus.

Everything before her was orange, and Lucy's first thought was that something had gone wrong with her vision. As things started to become clearer, she could see the bright orange bulb above her, shining down like copper mist. The light was dim, but still managed to send her head into a tailspin. The pain she felt increased by the second, and the room was swirling and shifting across her view.

She instinctively tried again to raise her hand, but no miracles had occurred. Cocking her head to the side was like an electric shock, but she managed to see her right hand and the leather straps that held it in place. She couldn't find the energy to turn to examine her left side, but she had no reason to think she would find anything different. She couldn't see her feet, but her inability to raise them spoke volumes.

The straps were coming from underneath a stainless-steel table like one that you'd find in an industrial sized kitchen or lab.

Or a morgue.

She was not lying flat, but at a steep angle; not fully upright, but close. The table must have a pivot function built in, and the strange angle was putting a great deal of pressure on her arms and shoulders. As Lucy's head cleared, the pain in her body became more prominent. She couldn't help but cry out in anguish, though she tried her best to hold back her agonized sound. Most of her upper body was on fire, and the straps were digging into her wrists so much that she was sure there was blood underneath the leather. Her fingertips were mostly numb, and the lurid shade of purple they were turning appeared black in the orange light.

Other than a cabinet to her right, she couldn't see much in the rest of the room, but there was no way to know what was behind her.

The only other notable sight was the curtain.

The orange glow of the room made it difficult to be sure, but Lucy had no doubt that it was red. A deep crimson curtain, almost certainly made of velvet, which ran the expanse of the wall directly in front of her. The wall was at least twenty-five feet long, if not longer, and it made her feel like she was on a stage; waiting patiently in her first position for the curtain to be drawn.

But there was no performance, no audience. Instead, there was complete silence, her own heavy breathing the only thing breaking up the quiet. Chills ran through her body, and her pain steadily grew. There was nothing she could do. Not yet. She had taken stock of her situation, and now all that was left was to wait. To lie there. Or more accurately, hang.

She desperately hoped that she would pass out again soon.

The pain in her head wasn't quite as intense when she woke again. She had stared into space for an unknown length of the time—occasionally sobbing, always praying. She felt rested, as if she had slept through the night, but her arms still felt like they were being slowly ripped from her body.

What time of day is it?

Looking around, Lucy found no changes in the room. The same orange glow filled the space, and it was starting to feel heavy. The light was pushing her down, causing her body to crumble, and with it, her resolve. She could not remember a time when she felt so completely helpless. Even years ago, when she felt trapped in her own home married to a man that controlled her very being, now felt like a distant cakewalk. No matter how hard she tried to keep it together and rationalize, she couldn't stop the fear from gripping her. Tears formed in her eyes once again, and she thought of her father and how ashamed he would have been of her now. He would have found her display of weakness pathetic. He would tell her to man-up, take charge, and take care of business.

There was no room for tears in this world.

She had learned so much from him in her youth, but his lessons had never covered this situation.

Kidnapped. Tied up. Alone.

How could she fight if she couldn't move?

No. She would bear the pain as she always had. Pain was just a reminder that she had shit to do, a little slap on the back that told her to get moving. The fear may have been strong now, but she had felt more agony than this. The stinging in her arms was no more than she would have felt training in the woods with her old man.

"This pain is nothing," she continued to repeat to herself. Eventually, the tears dried, and she felt exhausted. If she could move her legs, she would kick herself for exerting so much energy into something as worthless as lamentation.

"This pain is nothing."

Lucy scanned the room again, taking in the left side this time but still found nothing of consequence. Nothing she could use. She found it odd that she couldn't see any cameras. It would stand to reason that if someone wanted to go through the hassle of bringing her here, they would want to watch too. But there were no cameras, no little red power lights.

What if I was just left here to die?

When she heard the door open, her first thoughts were not joyous. She instinctively knew that whomever was behind her was not a savior. She would never have gotten that lucky.

The room suddenly brightened, and the orange glow was replaced by a softer, bluish light so bright that Lucy had to quickly shut her eyes. When she opened them again, black spots floated aimlessly around her corneas. Someone stood in front of her, but she couldn't make them out. She blinked repeatedly, desperately trying to find the person obfuscated by the dark spots, but only managed to see a faint outline standing in front of a wall of red.

"What's going on? Where am I, and who are you?" she asked, trying to stay calm.

There was no answer, and no sound of movement. When her eyes finally adjusted to the point of visual comprehension, she saw that the figure was indeed the man from before, but his appearance had changed.

He still wore the same expensive clothes, but the swagger that he had shown before was gone. He appeared now as a hollow, motionless shell, waiting for a small child to put a quarter in his slot so he could move again. His eyes were dark, appearing less like the window to his soul, and more like swamp water at night.

"Let me out of here! Let me go!"

"Pay attention to me!"

"You're sick. A sick fucking pervert!"

No reaction was given to her words. She expected him to lash out but he just he remained silent. The rising curiosity of what was happening caused her to stay her words as well. To be sure, she was frightened, but now her natural curiosity was piqued. If she had not been the one tied to the table, but rather an onlooker examining the situation, she would have been mesmerized. *What would he do to her?* Perhaps her eyes would have made contact with his own, and she would be sucked into oblivion with him.

Then, he moved.

His eyes came alive and met hers. Lucy's heart jumped at his transition from mindless automaton to responsive human being. He smiled slightly and looked as if he had seen her for the first time. He said nothing, but instead walked out of her field of view. Moments later, the light switched back to orange, and he was standing in front of her again. Luckily the change to orange was not as harsh on her senses.

Still, he said nothing.

"Please, just talk to me. Tell me what you want."

Ignoring her, he walked to the corner of the room and reached for a rope on the edge of the red curtain. He pulled downward and the fabric biblically parted, slowly revealing what was hidden beyond.

The curtain covered a massive sheet of glass, and on the other side was an elegantly decorated office. There were leather chairs, bookcases filled with elaborately bound tomes, expensive trinkets, and a mahogany desk that probably cost more than her car. Behind the desk, on the right wall, was a large window that showed her the sky.

The most dramatic sight in the office was the aquarium. It covered just over half of the opposite wall, and Lucy had never seen one so massive before. Swimming proudly in circles were three sharks. Not the size of those she had seen on the discovery channel, but every bit as menacing. Their teeth gleamed in the aquarium light as their permanent smiles passed by the front of the tank. Lucy had always been afraid of the ocean and sharks in general. The fact that these were contained in glass an entire room away wasn't much comfort.

The glass that separated her from the office was decidedly out of place. She felt like she was looking in on a zoo exhibit, observing the natural habitat of an office working human. A rich one.

You are the exhibit, Lucinda, not the office.

With the curtains fully drawn, the man looked out on the office with a satisfied expression. He looked back at Lucy and smiled again, wider this time. She got the distinct impression that he was proud to show her what lay beyond the glass. Then, he gave her a nod, as if he had just explained everything in perfect detail.

"Speak! Why won't you just tell me what is going on?"

The man frowned as he realized that he had not made himself clear, but instead of clarifying with words, he simply walked away. A few short steps, and he vanished again. Just a moment later, she heard a door open, then close. She didn't hear the sound of a locking mechanism. Perhaps he thought that there was no need for a locked door with her so thoroughly restrained, and for the moment, he was correct.

So, Lucy was left alone again to stare at an empty office and watch a trio of sharks endlessly make the same circular path around the tank. She called for help several times, but no one came. She watched the sunlight move slow and smooth across the office window. It was daytime. That was something at least.

A tidbit of knowledge to hold on to.

The sky had turned from blue to orange, nearly matching the color of her room. Lucy surmised that approximately five hours had passed. She could barely feel her fingers anymore, and the pain in her arms had become her new way of life. The air had grown steadily cooler, and her goose-bumped skin shuddered against the metal table.

She had called for help many more times, and her voice was hoarse. Occasionally she would erupt into a coughing fit that caused her entire body to writhe in punishment.

Lucy's will to keep her eyes open faded with the sun, and as the sky turned black, her eyelids grew heavy and closed. Her sleep was restless, her dreams malevolent.

She dreamed that she was in a wide open sea of white, and a presence was trying to kill her. She couldn't see or hear it, but she knew it was there, biding its time before ending her existence. She ran, but never was able to escape the whiteness, eventually succumbing to its overwhelming pressure, curling up, and melting away.

She again woke to light. The sun shone through the office window and burned her retinas but didn't seem to affect the orange glow around her. It was bright enough that she didn't immediately notice him.

The man, in a different suit than the last time, was sitting at the office desk. He had a stack of papers in front of him, and looked as if he was signing his name to them, one by one.

What was this?

He was just working. It was so normal. She was tied to a table, and this man was conducting business as usual on the other side of a giant pane of glass. The surreal nature of the moment was infuriating. Lucy called out to him.

"Hey!"

The man didn't move, but she didn't know if he didn't hear her, or if he was simply acting oblivious. She tried to call out again, but immediately started coughing. He didn't react. He turned page after page, signing them slowly, meticulously. She couldn't see the writing, but she could tell that he wasn't the type of person that scribbled his signature. He was too proud for that.

Lucy watched him work as the sun rose up and out of view. From time to time, a woman would come in and bring him something. A file. Some food. She wore the tightest of skirts, and there were several buttons undone on her blouse, reveal-ing cleavage that had to be enhanced by either an ambitiously padded bra or more surgical means. The first time the woman came in, Lucy had screamed with all the force she could muster with her wounded voice, but the girl never turned toward her, or gave any indication that she heard anything out of the ordinary. It dawned on Lucy that the glass must be a one-way mirror like the ones in police procedurals, and the room was most likely soundproofed.

There was no calling for help.

She felt simultaneously exposed and isolated.

Business continued on the other side of the glass which may as well have been the other side of the world. A world with sunlight and normalcy. Lucy could not fathom why she was made to watch the man, now slicing open envelopes with a gem crusted letter opener.

What was he getting out of it?

The sky again began to turn warm, and after finishing up a call, the man pressed the button on a call box nestled in between papers on his desk. The well-endowed woman, most likely a secretary, entered the office as she had many times throughout the day. This time, however, she brought nothing into the room with her and locked the office door behind her.

The man stood, loosened his tie, and pulled the shirt from the waist of his trousers. He had unzipped his pants and revealed himself before the secretary had even made her way across the room. She removed her blouse, leaving her expensive bra in place. The kind of bra that Lucy could never have afforded. All satin and lace with stitching so exquisitely sewn, a spider would bow her head in awe. The woman positioned herself in front of him in a manner that seemed as if she had done it a hundred times before.

As the woman's head bobbed up and down in his lap, the man slipped down into his chair, as if his spine could suddenly no longer support his weight. Without warning, the eyes that had previously been squarely focused on the secretary's work looked up at Lucy. She sighed and shook, suddenly filled with an intense fear. She had grown so complacent, just watching the show all day, that she had almost forgotten the danger she was in.

He was looking right at her; yet not. Lucy rationalized that there was no way that he could see her directly - not if she was correct about the one-way mirror – but he knew where she was. He looked sallow and defeated before smiling again.

He wanted her to see what he was doing.

He put his hand on the back of the woman's head, and grasping at her hair, pulled her down on him. She gave no resistance. Moments later, his eyes still fixed in Lucy's direction, he began to spasm. His smile turned into a contorted cavity of filth as he shoved his waist forward into the woman, whose head was held firmly in place until he was finished.

After he released his grasp on her, she rose, replaced her blouse, fixed her hair, and left.

The man sat heavily in his chair, his flaccid penis still exposed. He had not looked away from Lucy, but he now had the same hollow look he had shown her before. He made no move to button his trousers. In fact, he made no move at all.

It was dark before he finally snapped out of his haze. With a slightly confused look, he covered himself, then began to fill a briefcase with papers from the desk. Then, he tucked in his shirt and straightened his tie. He walked over toward Lucy, briefcase in hand, and rearranged his hair. When he checked his teeth, there was no longer any doubt that the other side of the glass was a mirror.

Then, he waved to her.

It was the kind of wave that a person would give from a front porch, wishing a family member well as they went off into the world. For the first time, it dawned on Lucy that she was going to be there for a long time. He was toying with her, and it was not going to end quickly.

"Goodbye," he was saying with that wave.
He would see her tomorrow.

CHAPTER 3

Lucy felt the cold wetness and smelled the sour odor before she opened her eyes. Last night, after stubbornly holding it to the brink of bladder explosion, she was forced to urinate. The act disgusted her, and what started as a vulgar warmth on her legs and crotch quickly devolved into a bitterly cold embarrassment.

The pain in her head had dissipated to almost non-existence, so at least she had that bit of positivity to start her day. A day of hanging, hurting, and being afraid. Right away, she began to lose her confidence. She remembered how it was before these days tied to a table. The mornings used to bring a new sense of possibility, and no matter how badly the previous day had been, when she opened her eyes snug in her bed, it was *all* possible. Reality always set in, but those oblivious morning moments were sacred to her, now gone.

When she finally opened her eyes, she saw that the curtains had been closed and the insipid orange glow was gone. She did not miss the hue. As the minutes ticked by each day, the color grew horrifying to her and affected her emotional state more than she would have thought possible; depriving her senses of what they expected. Unfortunately, the normal light also came with a closed curtain and the inability for her to see out the window. It probably didn't matter if it was day or night, but Lucy thought that it was somehow essential to mark the passage of time. If she lost track – more than she already had – then maybe the real world would disappear with time itself, leaving her as empty a shell as her kidnapper.

The change in lighting meant that he had come in while she was asleep, and that thought caused her skin to crawl. There was no telling what he may have done while she was zonked. He may not have even known himself, if her assessment of the man was correct. She didn't know where he went in those moments of haze he seemed to sink into, but she got the sense that they were nothing but a point of confusion for himself as well.

When Lucy heard the cough behind her, she jumped as much as her restraints would allow, again reminding her of the pain in her arms. She waited nervously for the man to show himself, but he didn't. Time passed, and still he didn't come around to her side of the room. Every now and then, she could hear a slight movement or clearing of a throat.

"If you're trying to scare me, you succeeded."

Nothing.

"Come on, just tell me why I am here," she said, beginning to feel like a broken record. "Are you going to kill me? Rape me?"

Lucy got no answer, and quit trying to acquire one. She let her head rest on the chilly metal, the icy sharpness of it no longer affecting her as bitterly as it had in the beginning. The tackiness in her mouth made her smack her lips, but she couldn't generate any new saliva. Her lips were cracked and burning; no surprise, considering how long she had gone without fluids. It was a surprise that her body was capable of making urine at all. She had made a concerted effort to not think of her hunger or thirst, but she was no longer able to ignore the facts.

I will die soon without water.

The fear that had been like a rollercoaster circumnavigating her heart, was receding. There was only so much that she could hold onto now, as she simply didn't have the energy to keep all of her emotions intact. Either he was going to do something to her, or he wasn't.

Clarity. She knew it was fleeting, and would be replaced soon enough with bewilderment, but she would relish it now. Like the majority of time she had been in her orange prison, she felt like she could drift back to sleep without any trouble. Maybe this time she would be fortunate enough to not wake at all, her body finally succumbing to dehydration.

It was a surprise when Lucy realized that she had already shut her eyes, and that was enough to make her pop her head back up, like a sufferer of an intense panic disorder suddenly aware of their impending death.

He was standing in front of her.

"Accidents happen," he said, "It's nothing to worry about."

His voice seemed alien, as if it were emanating from high above rather than the sadistic mouth of her warden. He seemed soft, almost childlike, and his eyes practically glittered as he looked at her. The change was off-putting, almost grotesque.

"I'm going to get you cleaned up, and everything will be just fine again. No reason to be embarrassed. What am I here for, if not to look out for you?"

"That wasn't an accident," she croaked. "I had no choice but to piss myself! In case you don't recall, let me remind you that you left me tied to this table for days."

His expression didn't falter; the smile on his face a monument to his lunacy. He walked out of view again, and when he returned he held a washcloth, sopping wet and dripping to the floor.

"Now, there is no reason to fret. We'll clean this right up, and everything can go back to normal. I know that you have had a bad day, but no one will ever know about this. I give you my word," he said, as he kneeled down before her. "I know that sometimes we fight, but I really think that we need to be supportive of each other now. It's the only way that we're going to get through this."

Lucy's mouth was agape as she looked down at the smiling man below her. Her neck strained as she looked, but she didn't notice the pain. He was insane. Had to be.

But how? What was the root of it all?

"What the hell are you talking about?" she asked. He was speaking as if he had known her far longer than the last hellish few days. She sorted through her distorted memories to try and find any that may include him, but came up blank. "I don't know who you are!"

"That isn't very nice. I'm trying here, aren't I? You never give me any credit."

As Lucy attempted to comprehend, the man reached up and took hold of her jeans, pinching them together and unbuttoning them. She tried to lurch her body as he unzipped the fly, and she winced as one of his fingers grazed her underwear. There was no escaping, but she continued to try, screaming at him to stop. Ignoring her pleas, he grasped the waist of her jeans and abruptly pulled them down her legs, nearly to her feet.

"Don't touch me, you fucking pervert! Let me go. Fuck!"

He had a frown on his face but kept mum. Instead, he began to run the washcloth against her inner thighs, moving slowly up and down. Tears moistened her cheeks, but she bit her tongue, not wanting to give him the satisfaction of knowing how much he had gotten to her. Fighting would get her nothing, so she went as limp as her frightened body would allow.

The man was gentle in the way he wiped her legs clean. Reverential.

When he slid his fingertips into the band of her underwear, Lucy tightened her eyes and bit her lip. The man pulled her panties down to her jeans. As he continued to wash her, she tried to go somewhere else in her mind, ignoring the wet towel pressed against her. She thought of the woods behind the house where she grew up. Lucy had spent so much time there with her father, and he had taught her everything among those trees. He taught her survival.

Do whatever you have to do to survive.

She stayed among the trees, listening to the distant sound of flowing water as he finished between her legs. Her skin tingled as it dried. He ran the washcloth across the crotch of her underwear and inside her jeans, then pulled both back up and fastened them again. She was just as soaked now as before, perhaps even more so, but she felt relief to know that most of it wasn't urine. Looking at the man, she couldn't tell if he had gotten sordid pleasure from cleaning her, or if he was honestly trying to help.

No! Don't start that shit, Lucinda. You will not feel for this psycho.

"That's better," he said, then tossed the rag into the corner of the room.

Her crotch and legs felt like ice as the damp fabric cooled. Lucy could feel her teeth begin to chatter slightly. She tried not to look at him, not wanting to see the eyes of the man who had just violated her.

But, she knew that he was still looking at her. She could feel his smile even if she couldn't see it.

"What do you want from me?" she asked as calmly as possible, still not looking in his direction. Instead, she focused in on the rag by the wall and let her vision blur. "Just tell me what you want."

"I've only ever wanted you to be proud of me. You know that."

"I don't know you. Do you understand?" she asked, as she began to slip into a frustration coma. He wasn't going to understand because he wasn't sane.

He didn't say another word to her, but disappeared behind her again. She screwed her eyes tight as he passed, still not willing to risk meeting his eyes. She had to be strong. Channeling her father, she willed herself to harden. He had done nothing to her that she couldn't get over. Not really.

"This pain is nothing," she whispered.

The fringes of her psyche still longed for the comfort of the trees. Lucy wanted to see her father, tough as nails as he was, standing in front of her twelve-year-old self. To hear his lectures on confronting the difficult things in life.

She hadn't always heeded his teachings, and that had proved disastrous. She had wised up, gotten stronger, but now she found herself in an unforeseeable horror show for which there was no lesson that could help her. She would have to pay attention and wait for any opportunity to present itself. Her kidnapper was unhinged, and if that told her anything, it was that mistakes would be made.

She had to be ready.

There was nothing that could be accomplished by confronting him, that was clear now. He would just ignore her. But if she tried to relate a little, then maybe she could get to him. Make him open up to her, and therefore reveal his weaknesses. Maybe. Despite all of the classes, she was no psychologist.

But you have to try, don't you?

It was then that the man returned, carrying two gallon-sized bottles of water and a small box. He placed everything on the floor directly in front of her, then removed the lid on one of the bottles.

"You must be absolutely famished," he said, as he raised the full bottle up towards her mouth. Without hesitation, Lucy opened wide as he poured with little regard for aim. The water splashed across her face and poured down her front, but she still managed to take several large gulps. Her mouth immediately began to feel better, but it was going to take much more for her lips to heal. She knew that the water that had drenched her shirt would soon become a frozen, stinging pain, but it was worth it.

She felt a quick pang of disgust when she thought about the hours ahead, when the need to pee could come around again.

Do I say thank you?

What a thought! In the real world, that wasn't a question that she would ever need to ask herself. Do you thank the man that tied you to a table and groped you for finally giving you a drink?

You do when you want to make sure he gives you another.

"Thank you," she said, almost inaudibly.

"Of course. You know that I only think of your comfort. Please don't hesitate to ask if you need more. How about some food?"

"Yes. Yes please."

He reached down to the box he had brought, and pulled the top free. Inside, were single wrapped bars of some kind. The man grabbed one and ripped open the package. He shoved it in front of her face, and Lucy leaned her head forward to take a bite. It was surprisingly tasty.

"I don't know if you know this yet, but the company has just started making these. Fifteen grams of protein per bar, and it doesn't taste like sawdust like all those other brands. I think you would be proud of what I have made here."

"They're good," she said, before taking another large bite.

"I really appreciate you saying so. There are plenty more when you get hungry, just help yourself."

"How am I supposed to do that?" she asked, chewing.

Not answering her, he pushed the protein bars and jugs of water toward the curtain with his foot. Lucy couldn't help but eye them longingly, and was already thirsty again.

"May I please have another drink of water?"

No answer.

He went behind her, and the light suddenly switched back to haunted copper. He went to the corner and drew the curtains open once again, then picked up the rag he had used to clean her. The office window was brightly lit, but the sun had risen high enough that she couldn't see it. It was midday, maybe a little later. She was suffering through what was at least her third day tied to the table.

He looked at her with black and sunken eyes, and this time she didn't look away.

"I'm so glad that we are back in each other's lives," he told her.

She wanted to scream. She wanted to rip his eardrums apart with anger, but it was no use. She calmed herself and attempted to play along.

"Yeah. So, can I get some water?"

The man just walked away and was gone from view again.

"Wait!"

"Yes?" he asked from somewhere behind her.

"What's your name?"

"What a silly question. My name is, and always has been, Edward."

Lucy heard the door open and close, and she was alone again. Alone and staring deeply into the eyes of two bottles of water. Begging them to come over and chat her up. They could have such a good time together.

"Buy me a drink?"

She was giggling and delirious. Her eyes were getting heavy, but she was too afraid to let them close. Edward was back in his fancy office, slicing open envelopes with his fancy letter opener.

His name was Edward.

Learn something new every day.

As the outside grew dark, the secretary came in. She made to assume the position, but he bent her over his desk instead. Lucy didn't watch this time, choosing to focus on the food and drink on the floor. She let her mind drift away with thoughts of sweet water on her tongue.

CHAPTER 4

Once upon a time, Lucy had been married, and she was quite happy in the beginning. She was able to ignore the many signs that her husband, Todd, wasn't what she had hoped. In the blink of an eye, a few drinks on the weekend became a few every day, and the lighthearted jokes morphed into vindictive dominance.

It took less than a year for Todd to hit her.

The first time was more of a shock than anything, and Lucy shrugged it off. He had promised to never again fall to that level of shame, but a few months later, it happened again. There wasn't an apology the second time, only a slew of words blaming *her* for what he had done.

From that point on, everything was her fault, the circumstances were irrelevant. Todd continued to drink and couldn't hold down a job for more than a few months. When he lost his job, it was always somehow his boss' fault or else her own.

She had given him too hard a time the day before and he hadn't slept.

She had upset him so much with her guilt trips that he hadn't the ability to concentrate.

She had angered him to the point that he couldn't be expected to care.

When he cheated, it was because she had not given him what he needed, and when he didn't come home, it was because she hadn't treated him as he deserved.

Sex became a violent activity as well, and the worst moments of her life came during what should have been the most pleasurable. Todd became unable to perform unless he was able to take his aggression out on her during lovemaking, and Lucy had been afraid for her life more than once.

She would often look back and try to pinpoint any moment in time that Todd had taken responsibility for his own faults, or shown real remorse for pain that he had inflicted, but there was nothing to find in those memories. She would then inevitably wonder why she hadn't seen what he was in those early days. Her rose colored glasses ended up being the catalyst for a change in life that blindsided her. It was confusion that caused her to stall, unable to make a choice.

Lucy had stayed with Todd for eleven years.

Reality hits hardest when we first wake up because the morning brings the most clarity.

Lucinda's situation had not gotten any better, and her new glowing orange home greeted her as she opened her eyes. Her vision was blurry at first, but clear or not, the room was still a waking nightmare. Her first instinct was to close them again—to try and go back to sleep. She was safe in sleep.

But, her father's influence kicked in, and she knew that she must focus. Find an opportunity where there was none. Pull a fucked up rabbit out of her hat.

When she finally lifted her head from the table, trying desperately to ignore the pain throughout her body, she saw Edward standing in the office. So close, yet so far. His body was right in front of her, and his right palm was pressed against the glass.

He seemed lucid this time, and she could see him squinting as if he was trying to see through the mirror to the other side.

To see her.

His lips parted, and his tongue slipped out a bit and hung slightly like a dog. There was pure lust in his eyes, and Lucy couldn't help but whimper as she imagined the ideas that must be in his head.

Why hasn't he raped me?

A dark thought, but a valid question. If Edward was getting off on this and if the whole thing was about his perverted power trip, then why hadn't he done anything to her? She couldn't be sure what he had done while she was knocked out, but she didn't feel as if she had been violated in that way. The one time he had touched her seemed out of pity, or even compassion.

His proclivities must have been more complicated. Maybe sex wasn't what he got off on, and he needed this voyeuristic sadism to get his jollies.

Stop it, Lucinda! Why are you spending time trying to analyze the man? He is a fucking pervert, and that's the end of it.

Edward reached down between his legs with his left hand and latched onto the bulge there. Lucy wanted to look away, but just like the scene of a car accident, it was difficult to stem curiosity. He rubbed himself over his slacks, never removing his other hand from the glass.

Was he trying to touch her?

He began to unclasp his pants but halted when the door to his office opened. The secretary had brought food. She looked at him for a few moments but he didn't turn back to see her. She crossed the room, looking over at him a couple of times, then set the food on the desk and hurried out, never speaking a word.

Despite herself, Lucy chuckled. In the secretary's view, her boss was just staring at himself in the mirror with his hand on his crotch. She thought that even for a slut like the secretary, it must have been an odd sight. After the office door closed,

Edward looked back at his lunch, and when his eyes returned to the mirror, his hands remained chaste. He didn't give Lucy another glance as he sat and ate his meal.

As she watched the sharks circle, Lucy's body shivered. Not from the cold, but from the sudden remembrance that she had not looked away. Edward was touching himself, and she had watched. If the secretary had not come in, and he had continued, would she have averted her eyes? Would she have been disgusted?

Would I have gotten turned on?

The idea that she may have enjoyed his display, even a little, made her sick. Her stomach churned and ached, and it was not just from the lack of food. She honestly didn't know if she would have watched, and that was disturbing. She thought the secretary a slut, but what about her?

Hours of painful boredom later, Edward abruptly stood from his chair, jostling her from the numbing trance she had perfected. He had been sitting with his paperwork the whole day, and that had left Lucy with nothing to watch but the space between.

Edward exited through the side door, and she knew it would only be a few minutes before he entered her room. She heard the door open and he rushed over to the water bottles, not bothering to close the door behind him. He splashed some water across her face in a half-assed attempt at giving her a drink, soaking her shirt more than her mouth once more. Lucy licked her lips and around her mouth, desperate for every drop.

He set the bottle down with no regard for her plight, then took a seat on the floor; his back pressed against the glass. He sighed a loud, desperate, attention-grabbing sigh, though Lucy hadn't a clue from where else he thought attention would come besides his captive audience.

"It's hard you know? I'm tired of it all," he said, "I push the papers and make the decisions, but there is no glamour in it. Nothing to fuel my pride. I used to think that running the company was what I needed. I thought it would make a difference. But money and power get old just like anything else."

Edward rattled out the words as if they had been prepared and delivered many times before. Almost like he had chosen those specific words to define himself but had got bored with them long ago.

He reached into the inner pocket of his suit jacket and pulled out a pack of cigarettes. Using a book of matches that he had stashed in the cellophane wrapper, he lit one. His first drag was deep enough that Lucy wondered if it would ever cease. He exhaled the smoke into the air in front of her and the coughing commenced. She had always abhorred the smell of cigarettes, even during that four-month window when she was twenty— when she had grand aspirations of enlightenment in the human condition and thought that smoking would help. She never could get the hang of the act and the smell was a deal breaker.

Edward, ignoring her coughs, said, "Everybody always wants more, but what happens when you get to the end of the line? When there is no more to want?" He took another deep drag, and this time Lucy tried to hold her breath while the cloud swirled in the orange light around her, slowly dissipating. "You know, sometimes I think I might be cracking up. I think that maybe I don't have a clue what's really going on. I know, it doesn't make sense, right? I *create* what is going on. I built it all, and it all runs because I make it run. Still, shit happens, and I am not sure how it got that way. Like you, for example."

Lucy was surprised to hear him address her directly. Until now, his words had been nothing but a bag of confusion for her. It was a toss-up in her mind whether or not she should say.

She wanted answers, but knew there was a risk that he would just go silent again.

"Are you saying that you kidn...brought me here accidentally?" she asked.

"Nothing is accidental. I had a reason; I can be sure of that, at least."

He finished his cigarette and put it out on the floor, leaving the smoldering butt where it lay, then stood back up. He turned his back to her and looked out on his office.

"From here," Edward said, "It's like I don't exist over there. As long as I stay in this world, that one stands still. I'm sure that's why I built this in the first place. I took you from that world and brought you into this one with me. You ought to be grateful. That world – isn't worth it."

"I don't understand this place – this world," she said.

"You will eventually. I did, and so will you."

He didn't look back at her, but she could hear the difference in Edward. This version of him was almost normal. A man finding his way. He appeared softer, as if his stresses had dripped away in the copper glow, and what remained was a ghost of Edward past. A phantom that had shed its insanity and made peace with eternal confusion.

As they both looked in on the office, the door opened and the secretary came in. She walked over to the desk and grabbed a couple of files, but instead of leaving again, she looked around the room for any potential prying eyes, then sat down in Edward's chair. The woman had a hard time lifting her legs, as tight as her skirt was, but eventually managed to prop both of her feet on the desk and lean back. The chair dwarfed her like a child queen on a throne.

"Oh, this is perfect!" Edward said, now giddy. He ran around the back of the room, and a moment later, Lucy could hear the voice of a woman singing quietly, and it took a moment for her to realize that it was the secretary.

Edward came back around. "Intercom I set up a while ago," he said. "We can hear her, but she can't hear us. My assistant – Bonnie."

He had an anticipatory look on his face that was much like watching a roulette wheel spin after an obscenely overzealous bet on black.

The woman – Bonnie - was singing a song that Lucy didn't recognize, though it was obvious that she didn't know all of the words. After repeating a couple of lines over and over, she eventually stopped and began to talk. "Oh, yes sir, Mr. Wolcroft. Anything you say, Mr. Wolcroft. Oh, you want me to suck your flaccid cock again, no problem at all."

Lucy could see Edward tense up at that last bit, but he softened soon after.

"Fuck you, Eddy!" Bonnie yelled. Then, as if she got a sudden impression that she could get caught at any moment, stood and began to leave. She turned back to straighten the chair into the same position it was in before she sat, grabbed the files from the desk, then left at a very quick pace, almost running.

"Bonnie is a character, isn't she? I'll have to punish her for that display." Edward said, turning back to Lucy. "She has done it before, but I always see. You know what? I think I am going to leave that intercom on for you. I don't know why I didn't think of it before. It ought to be more entertaining than silence while I figure out what to do with you."

He tapped on the glass, at first in a constant rhythm and then in a haphazard rendition of "Ode to Joy."

"One way mirror," he said, "Obviously. You want to hear something funny? One way mirrors only work when the window side is dark, and the mirror side is lit up. That means that if someone were to come up real close, they would be able to see the orange glow behind the mirror. If they looked real, real close, they could even see you. Isn't that exciting?"

He dangled the information like a hooked worm in summer waters, letting it float out there, threatening hope.

"If you don't know why I am here, then why don't you let me go?"

"Because, I'm not a fool. You won't be going anywhere at all."

He reached up and touched her hair, running his fingers down the length of it several times. He smiled, but it faded. His hand dropped down to his side, and Edward once again had a dead stare. Lucy's heart began to beat faster. The orange glow on Edward's face didn't seem to reflect in his eyes. They appeared as two black holes, eating the light. She was drawn into them, and it frightened her.

"Get away from me!" she shouted "Just go away, and leave me alone."

Edward didn't listen, and when he finally did move again, he wasn't the same. He looked at her lovingly. Longingly. His face seemed to pulse in the light, forcing her to see into his being. Lucy knew it was just a trick of the orange, but sight was her only reality while strapped to the table.

"I'm doing my best," he said. "Please have faith in me. It won't be long, and you'll be proud. I know you will. Despite everything, I still love you."

Lucy didn't say a word, and she knew that he wouldn't hear her anyway.

"I know. It's hard. He's vicious. But, just a little while longer, okay?"

She nodded, though for the life of her, she couldn't fathom why.

"We have to get ready now. Daddy will be home soon."

Daddy?

Edward said nothing else, but ran his fingers through her hair once more. She heard the click of the door as he left. She waited for a few minutes to make sure he had really gone before she finally relaxed. She hadn't noticed just how tense her body had become until she let it slump against the table and her muscles felt like a lava flow, burning her to the core.

"Fuck!" she screamed, hoping that swearing at the air would make her feel better.

It didn't.

Later, Edward returned to his office, and it was business as usual. He flipped through files, talked on the phone, and gave instructions to Bonnie. It was surreal to hear him, even more so because he was so damned normal. He was acting like any other person running a business. Lucy couldn't fathom how he could move back and forth so freely between these "two worlds" he'd alluded to.

Her arms were aching. It was strange how she could actually forget the pain for long stretches of time. She was adapting, and that was something to fear. She could not resign herself to a lifetime of – this.

As the sky darkened, Edward packed his briefcase, but instead of getting up to leave, he sat back in his chair. His body slumped into the cushion in nearly the same way that Bonnie's had, though his feet remained on the floor. There he sat, not moving much. Lucy didn't think that he was in one of his trances, though he was staying relatively still for a long time, only sitting up a little when Bonnie entered the room.

"If there is nothing else today, I'll be going Mr. Wolcroft."

"I need you to stay for just a bit longer."

"Ok, no problem," the assistant said, as she put her bag down on a chair and let her hair down. As she walked toward him, she began to undo some of the buttons on her blouse. Lucy had seen this play out without sound, but now that she could hear, it seemed ceremonial.

"Where would you like me today, sir?"

Instead of answering, Edward rose and walked over to the woman. She stood before him and made as if to kneel, but he stopped her. They locked eyes, and then he slapped her. His arm swung up and into her right cheek so fast that neither Bonnie, nor Lucy, saw it coming. The woman leaned hard to the left and put her hand to her cheek. She didn't scream, but began to tear up. When she rose again, her mascara was smeared across her reddened cheek. Lucy was worried that he would hit her a second time, but instead he stepped to the side and motioned to his desk.

"Bend over."

Bonnie, still crying, pulled her skirt and underwear down to her ankles, then bent herself over the front of Edward's desk, pushing several things to the side in the process. Edward removed his suit jacket, then positioned himself behind her. As he began to unfasten his belt, Lucy looked away.

She stared into the wall to her right, still hearing Bonnie's quiet sobbing. Then she heard her grunt, and the unmistakable sounds of sex. Bonnie was faking; that was clear. She was overdoing her part to an extreme degree.

"Yeah, take it. You like that, don't you?" Edward bellowed.

"Yes, Mr. Wolcroft. Give it to me harder."

Bonnie's voice was hollow, with no real intensity or desire in her words. Still, it seemed to spur Edward on, and Lucy found that she could no longer look away. What she saw was both erotic and comical. He was thrusting into her and spanking her hard, each slap ricocheting from the intercom to Lucy's ears. Bonnie was flailing her body as if she had never been fucked so good in her life, but her face was devoid of pleasure. Edward had a maniacal look. A look of evil pride.

"Tell me I'm the best. Tell me that nobody fucks you like I do."

"Nobody could ever fuck me as good as you, Mr. Wolcroft. You're the best I have ever had. I'm such a lucky girl."

41

Lucy continued to watch, and despite herself and the ridiculousness of the situation, she became aroused. The sight of Bonnie bent over the desk, exaggerated as it was, titillated her senses. She bit her lip lightly.

No!

What the hell was she doing? Suddenly, her stomach threatened to release its contents, but there was simply nothing to evacuate. She dry-heaved several times, ashamed of what had happened. How could she find the display erotic? She felt like she was changed. A few days tied to a table and a couple of peculiar conversations was enough to flip a switch in her brain.

She had to get out of there, and soon. Otherwise, there may be nothing left of her to escape.

CHAPTER 5

"Let me go, you piece of shit!"

The voice was male, and a lot of noise was coming from behind Lucy. She strained to hear, to ascertain what was going on. Loud thuds, like bodies slamming into hard walls, and yelling that seemed to reverberate. Had someone come for her? Would she be saved from this hell?

"I will fucking...kill you...I..."

Another thud, louder than the others. Then quiet. Lucy looked left, then right. A desperate attempt to see something that she knew was out of view. The light above was fluorescent, and the curtains were closed. Her head was light and she would be covered in sweat if not for the lack of fluids in her body.

She heard the door open, then rattle as it banged against the wall, followed by the sound of dragging. Something heavy. There was a final thud before Lucy heard Edward sigh. She knew his voice, even if it was just the expelling of air.

Her hopes of rescue collapsed into a heap of depression. As she closed her eyes, Lucy wanted to cry again, but her body was too dehydrated to waste the tears. As she was about to raise the nerve to call out to her captor, she felt a sting in her neck, just as she did on the last night she had been free. Her vision blurred, and she slurred out the word, "Why?"

Lucy heard the dragging sound again as she drifted off.

Lucy sat on her favorite rock as her father tied the rope. He had made it himself with brown vines gathered from the forest. She had helped him collect enough to make a long enough rope to hoist the canopy. He looked at her and nodded. It was time for her to climb.

So desperate to show him that she could make it up the tree without a problem, Lucy dropped her knife in a clumsy grab for a branch that she should have known right away wasn't strong enough to hold her weight.

"What now? Do you come back, or do you keep going?" her father asked.

Keep going.

Go back, you need that knife.

You can do it, just keep going.

Deciding to try and tie off the canopy without her knife proved incorrect. She needed to cut the line to tie more knots. While trying to pierce the thick, woody vine with the pocket knife that her father had given her for her seventh birthday, she slipped and fell. She and the canopy dropped to the ground, her head rang like a gong as she landed; her eyes suddenly dark.

The blurry image of her hovering father was the first thing Lucy saw when her eyes began to correct. Even in the hazy blur, she could see his disappointment.

"I should have come back for the knife," she said.

"A little late, isn't it?"

"Yes," she said, as she sat upright and dusted herself off. Lucy returned to her rock and sat solemnly.

"Feeling sorry for yourself isn't going to accomplish anything. You can quit, or you can persevere. What is it that you are going to do?"

"Persevere."

"You sure? 'Cause it don't matter how old or small you are. You may be six years old today, but in a blink of an eye you'll be sixty. The rules will still be the same, best to learn them now."

"Yes, Daddy."

"Good. Now pick up that knife and start climbing."

Her head was wrecked. It felt as if the veins that wrapped her skull had been filled with gunpowder, and each breath sent a flame through them. She couldn't bring herself to open her eyes again, not just for the pain, but because she had no way of knowing what she would find. Even if everything in the room had stayed the way it had been, Lucy didn't know if she could face that orange light again.

Her mind's eye visualized a clock, and as she watched the seconds tick, the smell of cigarette smoke caught in her nostrils.

He was here.

Still, she kept her eyes shut tight. Maybe he hadn't noticed that she had awoken. If she just kept quiet as the dead, he may go away.

God, Lucinda, what the hell are you doing? Don't let him beat you. Don't let him have more control than he already does.

Begrudgingly, she opened her eyes, and found the curtain still closed; the orange light still sleeping. Edward was hunched over on the ground, holding his knees to his chest, and blowing smoke in all directions as he slowly shook his head. From here, Lucy could see that his eyes were bloodshot; his hair disheveled. There was a pile of butts next to him on the floor, a few still smoldering. As he finished the cigarette in his mouth, he dropped it in the pile and lit another.

"Can I have some water?" she asked.

"No."

He took a deep drag, then looked up at her. "Fine, okay."

With the cigarette dangling from the corner of his mouth, Edward stood, grabbing a jug of water on the way up. He seemed disoriented, and moved like an amateur tightrope walker working without a safety net for the first time.

"Stood up too fast, I guess," he said, then lifted the open jug to her lips. This time, he actually tried to pour the water into her mouth, and Lucy got a healthy shot of life before Edward's arm began to shake and he dropped the jug back to the floor. When it hit, some of the water splashed across the smoldering cigarettes, causing them to sizzle and sputter smoke in their demise. He peeled open a protein bar and fed it to her in large chunks, not waiting for her to chew completely before shoving another hunk in her face. Then, he collapsed back to the floor and lit another cancer stick.

"Thank you," she said, without hesitation.

He waved his hand dismissively, cocked his head back, and blew a steady stream of smoke into the ceiling. He looked to Lucy like he was on the verge of collapse, and she wondered how often – if at all – he slept.

"Sometimes I just have to make a choice, and it's that simple. Then I have to go with it – whatever happens," Edward said, though not to her specifically. "Doesn't matter if I don't know why, I just have to deal."

He performed another cigarette exchange.

"I guess you'll have someone to talk to. Can't imagine he will be very pleasant though,"

Lucy was contemplating the fact that she never saw him smoke in the office, so it took a moment to realize that he was now talking to her.

"What do you mean?" she asked.

He reached his hand up, cigarette between his fingers and pointed to Lucy's left. What she saw would have made her jump if she had the means. Where once was nothing but empty space, was now another table like hers with a man strapped to it in the same fashion. He was not moving, and for a moment, Lucy thought that he might be dead. On closer inspection, his chest was filling with air, albeit at a snail's pace.

"Who is he?"

"That isn't important at all."

Once Edward finished his current cigarette, he reached into the pack and found that the cupboard was bare. He crumpled the pack as he stood, this time managing to stay rigid, then threw it down into his previous mess. He crossed the room, the light flickered and changed, then slowly meandered to the corner and opened the curtain.

It was midday. How many days had it been? Five? Six? The concept was a blur now. Her arms and shoulders were numb, and she couldn't feel her hands at all. The rest of her body felt cold inside. The feeling one gets just before an illness overtakes them, or whatever a cadaver must feel while lying patiently in the drawer.

Edward looked out onto his office, and Lucy watched as his shoulders slumped down, his hands relaxed by his sides. He appeared thinner, elongated. She was witnessing the change from one Edward Wolcroft to the other. Lucy wouldn't say that he had multiple personalities, as he remained a version of himself whenever he entered this state. It was delusion that changed him.

Stop it! Let it go.

Again, she was analyzing; attempting to figure him out. It was a habit that she was never able to kick, even after she had dropped out of college. Once she met Todd, the psychology degree she had been working on didn't seem so important anymore. The man of her dreams—now a frequent resident in her nightmares. If only she had been able to analyze herself, maybe her decisions could have made more fucking sense.

The man that stole her and forced her into this position didn't deserve her empathy. He was a waste of effort. Still, she knew no other way. She was beginning to know the man, and with that came a desire for understanding. There was never any grey area for Lucy, and she was always all in or completely apathetic. Stockholm Syndrome was Psych 101. Baby stuff. Still, she couldn't help but think that knowing what made Edward tick might give her some sort of advantage later.

Later. What a concept that is! What do I really expect to happen – later?

Lucy was wrapped up in her head when Edward turned around, startling her. His smile was back, as was his look of empathy. He reached down and grabbed another protein bar, this time feeding it to her in easily manageable bites.

"It's going to be a tough time now that Dad is home. I promise that I will stand up to him. I will! I just don't want to hurt."

She had already begun to tune him out as she chewed. The protein bar was something she could understand, and far more important than Edward's ravings.

"I don't want you to hurt either, Mother."

Whoa! What?

It was finally out there. Lucy knew that he was seeing her as someone that she wasn't, and while "mother" was always a possibility, she had been trying to deny it. The idea made her furious, made her want to scream until Edward's ears bled, but the logical part of her knew that she should play along with his fantasies – that would be the best way to find a way out of this mess. Again, she would choke back emotion in the name of composure and clear thought.

"Your mother wants you to let her down from this table," she said, lacing her voice with maternal authority.

"Oh, stop playing, Mom. This is serious. Dad is home. He may be sleeping now, but he will wake up. You need to stay strong."

"Edward, please listen to me. You need to let me go."

He looked at her as if she had said absolutely nothing. Was he even hearing the words she said, or was he just dubbing in his own voiceover to her moving mouth? Pretending wasn't working and wasn't going to work. She wouldn't escape by playing house. Her fury was boiling up inside her, and against all rationality, Lucy snapped at him.

"Hear me, you fucked up shit-bag," she said, as deliberately as she could. "Hear these words. I am NOT your mom!"

Edward's face contorted into one of fear and submission. Had he heard her?

"I don't know why you have to be so hurtful all the time. I do the best I can, and I love you," Edward said, and then reached up to caress her face. Lucy threw her head to the side, his touch diseased.

He sighed, then smiled again. She hadn't even made a dent in his psyche. He was trapped in there, just as she was trapped in this pumpkin-colored hell.

After he left, she cried. This time, she didn't bother stopping the tears.

As the sharks swam, their pattern never changed. The largest one had a rip in its left pectoral fin. The shark's expression never changed, and it never seemed to grow bored. Its life was simple. Serene.

The inside of Lucy's body was growing colder. Sickness was on her doorstep with the hard sell and her mind felt like it was stuck in first gear. Each time she focused on something, she found it harder and harder to snap back. Small movements caught the corner of her eye only to vanish before she could turn her head. The shadows that the orange glow created moved more often than they should. The lack of water was getting to her, and she knew that she couldn't go on like this. She would grow weaker until she withered, body and mind.

The man beside her had not risen, but his body had been twitching for a while.

Who is he?

Other than the sharks and sleepy, twitchy man, Lucy had only Edward to watch. He sat upright, no curve to his back at all, his hand moving smoothly across the papers before him, and Lucy could see the side of him that was so intoxicating when they first met. He was a commanding person, but he had finesse. As she listened in on his phone calls, he never wavered in his speech, and always seemed to get exactly what he wanted from whomever was on the other end of the line.

The sharks kept swimming and she wished they would all just stop, turn, and swim the other way. Lucy was mesmerized.

It was the screaming that broke her trance. The sound startled her, but she avoided looking in the man's direction. She had to maintain control of her own terror, she couldn't be responsible for his too.

"What the?" the man asked. "My head is pounding. Where the fuck am I?"

Lucy had her eyes closed, ignoring him. She focused in on her thirst, felt the cracks in her lips with her tongue. She imagined the taste of ice cream in her mouth, and the feel of rose petals between the tips of her fingers.

"Lady? What the fuck is happening?"

She smelled cinnamon bread baking in the oven.

"Can you fucking hear me?"

The cool breeze by the shore at dusk.

"Lady!"

Lucy's eyes opened. The man was not going to go away.

"This pain is nothing," she said.

"What? Are you right in the head? Why the fuck are we tied to these tables? And what is that?" he asked, motioning with his head toward the glass. He yelped in pain from the movement.

"Am I right in the head? How would I know? The man sitting at that desk tied you to that table. You're his daddy."

"His what? I don't have fucking kids, lady."

"You say 'fuck' too much."

"Oh, excuse the fuck out of me! Tell me what is going on."

"Look around, and you'll know as much as I do." Her words sounded disconnected. Lucy was on autopilot. "I've been here a while now, and nothing has changed except for you. He believes I am his mother, and you are his father. Don't ask me why."

Moments later, the man was screaming again. Lucy was amazed at the high pitch he was able to achieve. He called for help multiple times before Lucy informed him that it wouldn't work. He continued anyway.

"No one is coming, and you'll just lose your voice. We need to be able to talk to each other, so don't let that happen."

"I don't need to talk. I need to get the fuck out of here!"

With every synapse she could fire, Lucy gathered her thoughts and focused.

"You think I want to stay? You aren't getting loose no matter how much you squirm, and nobody will hear you. The room is sound proofed, and that is a one-way mirror. The only way out for either of us is communication. We put our heads together, and we'll come up with something."

The man was crying. In the real world, Lucy would have thought him juvenile. In Hell, it was completely different.

Edward kept working, and the sky grew dark. Behind him, raindrops began to hit the window and lightning strobed the clouds.

"It's shock," she said. "It will wear off, and you'll get used to it. That's when we need to think this through. There has to be a way out. Edward is insane; he'll crack."

The man stopped blubbering for a moment to ask, "Edward? Is that his name?"

"Yeah. Edward Wolcroft. I'm Lucy. Who are you?"

"*The* Edward Wolcroft? The billionaire Wolcroft?"

"I would imagine so. I don't keep up with that sort of thing, but he has sharks, so I imagine he has money. Now, what's your name?"

"Woltech. You've never heard of them? They make everything."

"The name doesn't ring a bell, and neither does yours, as you haven't told me yet."

"Sorry. Roger. Roger Clifton."

The new roommates watched Edward work from the comfort of their tables. Lucy's mind blurred along with her eyes as Roger Clifton continued to cry.

The sharks went round and round; the rain came down, down, down.

CHAPTER 6

"Wake up!"

Roger was yelling at her, and Lucy knew that she should wake, but the thought of never-ending sleep enticed her. She could feel her insides drying out. If Edward showed up to offer her a drink— could she refuse? Her death would take his satisfaction away. Let him find a new mother.

"Come on, lady, wake the fuck up!"

"My name is Lucy."

"Whatever. You wanted to talk, so let's talk."

Get it together, Lucinda!

Her father was in her mind again, forcing her to action. She had to be stronger and felt ashamed for trying to give in. When she opened her eyes, she could see the image of her father before her. For a split second, he was there, bathed in fluorescent light and frowning at her silence.

"Ok," she said, "Let's talk."

"How long have you been here?" he asked.

"I don't know for sure. I try and keep time when the curtains are open, but," she looked forward and tilted her head, "As you can see, they are closed a lot. Not to mention, all the times that I am completely knocked out. I think that I've been here about a week, give or take a day."

Those few words alone were taxing and Lucy already felt short of breath.

"Fuck," said Roger.

"Yeah. Fuck."

"Why am I here?"

"That's the million-dollar question. We are here, because Edward Wolcroft is a crazy person." Lucy tried to stretch her neck, but it would barely budge. "There are different sides to him. Sometimes he is a coherent business man, and others he is a babbling, needy child. When he is like that, he thinks I'm his mother, and now that you're here, he has both his parents. If you're wondering what he is going to do with us, I really don't know."

She tried again to move her neck, tilting it to her left side as far as it would go. Finally, a loud pop, and she could look around the room again.

"And, what is the deal with the window?" Roger asked.

"Well, that's the show. We get to see Mr. Wolcroft run his business and fuck his secretary. We've got the best seats in town."

Lucy smiled, but Roger wasn't amused. He didn't seem like the sort that would make a joke in a dire situation, but Lucy couldn't help herself, especially when she was lacking in energy. In real life, she always got her goofiest just before bed.

"What do you do? For a living I mean," she asked.

Roger went berserk. He began to rock his body back and forth with fury. His skin was turning red; his eyes were bugging.

"What does it matter what I do? How can you be so calm about this! Making jokes – what is wrong with you?"

He tossed himself so hard that the table was starting to move against the floor, creating a horrible shrieking sound that reverberated through the room. The table began to tilt, and despite Lucy's warnings, he didn't stop.

The table fell to the floor in slow motion before her eyes, causing such an explosion of noise that she was sure the entire building must have heard; soundproofing or not. The left corner of the metal table had hit the left wall, causing the table to flip around. Lucy could no longer see Roger, only the hydraulic mechanism beneath the table.

All he had to look at now was the corner of the room.

"You ok?" she asked.

"Fuck off."

Time passed. Roger didn't speak. Lucy felt alone again, even though she could hear him breathe. Her own breathing had gotten very shallow, and from time to time, she would gasp and wonder if that was it for her.

"Listen, I joke because this whole situation is insane, and the jokes keep me from going that way myself."

"I have to pee," Roger said.

"Yeah. Better go ahead and go right where you are. There are no intermissions in this show."

"It's a goddamn shit show. Where the fuck is he anyway? You said he gave you food."

Lucy was growing weaker by the second like weights were tied to her limbs, pulling her deep into a deep dark well, but she did her best to pay attention to Roger's ramblings. As annoying as the man was, it was the best conversation she had come across in some time. Her head was spinning and the strange phantom movements continued, now taking the general shapes of images from her past. It didn't matter how many times Lucy told herself they were just hallucinations; they still freaked her out. They were getting worse and she knew it.

She kept her eyes closed, which helped some.

"Maybe he took the day off. Besides, he doesn't always give me food. Only when he is Edward number One. Edward number Two doesn't comprehend any needs, he's too busy fantasizing about perfection."

She had spent a long time explaining to Roger what he could expect from their captor. Calling him Edward One and Edward Two seemed the simplest way. In return, Roger had finally opened up a little. He was in the flooring business-tile, wood, carpet- that sort of thing. He had a wife, Jennie, waiting for him at home but according to Roger, she wouldn't be holding her breath.

"I'm a shit husband. Always have been. It'll take her a few days before she starts to worry...or celebrate," he had said.

Roger had one child with his first wife, but he had given up custody when she wanted her new husband to adopt the kid. Telling the story, Lucy could tell that he was quietly devastated by that decision.

"It is for the best. The kid needs better than me."

That was all there was to know about him, he had told her.

Everything about a person can be summed up in a few simple facts.

Lucy had yet to tell him much about her own life, but Roger hadn't asked. She thought it impolite to force her story on unwilling parties, but more than that; she was fading, and every word threatened to slur and die before it reached his ears.

"I can't feel my arm," he said.

"So you've said many times. Neither can I. You'll get used to it."

"I have to get the fuck out of here. I'll be a better person. I'll be a better husband."

Lucy knew this wasn't true. If Roger made it out of here, his spots wouldn't change any more than hers would. Trauma gives us an illusion that we can be something we aren't, but she couldn't tell him that.

"Yeah. You'll get out. Just be strong, we'll find a way."

As much as she wanted to keep on her father's good side, Lucy was quickly losing heart. She didn't see any opportunity before her, and if Edward didn't give her water soon, it wouldn't matter. She had not been released from the table since she arrived, so no opportunities to exploit had yet presented themselves to her. Right now, she wasn't sure she would recognize one anyway. She couldn't do it anymore. Not now. Maybe tomorrow.

Finally giving herself over completely to hopelessness freed her; let her relax her mind. It felt euphoric to let go of hope. Roger was crying again, but she didn't care. She couldn't take care of him. Lucy was free now.

She could sleep.

Lucy was drifting in and out, it frustrated her. All she wanted was to sleep, but something kept waking her. Roger snored in the corner, but that wasn't the problem. It was her stomach cramping up and the wheeze that came with each breath. Hunger was preventing rest and, that seemed ironic somehow.

Lucy tensed as she heard the door open and close, but relaxed when she realized that it wasn't the door to her room that made the sound, but the office door over the intercom. The curtain was closed, but she could hear giggling, some sighing. Kissing. Slurping.

"Roger, wake up!" she rasped.

A moment later, "What? What is it?"

"I don't know yet. Just hush and listen."

The sounds of lust continued, getting louder and more passionate. There was rustling, the sound of something heavy hitting the floor, shoes tossed aside, and clothes discarded in haste.

Occasionally, Lucy could hear words buried within the pants and moans.

"Just throw it."

"No, on the desk."

"Oh God, yes. Fuck me."

The male voice was not Edward's. Bonnie had brought in a mystery man, and Lucy couldn't help but get turned on by the sound. Edward wasn't involved, so there was no guilt in the pleasure she derived. She was free to enjoy the sounds, despite the situation. No matter how bad things were, could a person keep up misery the entire time?

Roger wasn't saying anything, but his snores had ceased. She couldn't hear him breathing at all, though she could hear her own raspy breath grow more rapid.

The hidden sex only lasted a few minutes, and Lucy sighed as the couple finished. Despite the shortness of the activity, Bonnie seemed to have had quite the time. After, Lucy heard the sound of a lighter flick, along with the rustling of garments.

"Thanks, but why in here?"

"Because, fuck my boss," said Bonnie.

"I thought you said at the bar that you loved your job."

The sound of zipping jeans.

"I do. I barely have to do any work, and there is no one around to bother me. I get paid a stupid amount. My boss can suck it though."

"You are his secretary?"

"Assistant, and yes. I also perform other duties as assigned."

"You mean...?"

"Yeah, but it's no big deal. The guy can't get it up ninety-five percent of the time anyway. He just rams his little limp dick against my crotch and makes me tell him he's the best. Sometimes I pretend to suck him off. On the rare occasion that he does manage to get an erection, he always makes me stop. It's weird."

"Why does he make you stop?" the man asked.

"No idea," she said, as Lucy heard the sounds of shuffling papers. "Hey pick that up and put it back on the desk. Anyway, it's like he changes or something. Like he feels guilty for getting it up."

"Your boss sounds like a freak. You want to go get another drink?"

"Nah, I'm gonna go hook back up with my girlfriends. It was nice meeting you though."

"Wait..."

The door closed before Lucy could hear the rest of their conversation. She thought of that first time that Edward stared at her as Bonnie went down on him, now knowing that it was all an act. Why had he done that?

Was it to make me jealous? That would line up with the classic Oedipus Complex. He wants to fuck me – his "mom." I won't, so he tries to persuade me in any way he can.

She didn't even try to stop herself from analyzing him. Just as she hadn't the energy to think when needed, she was too drained to prevent herself from thinking when her brain chose to. Having thoughts was easier than forcing them away.

Edward had his mother right here waiting for him. He could have her whenever he wanted; it was only a matter of time.

Eventually he would come for her.

The voice Lucy heard then was more frightening than any of the things that had happened to her in this room. There was no denying the tone, the inflection. It was him.

"Yes, he will come for you. You deserve it, bitch."

Todd, her long dead husband, spoke the words directly into her ear. He was close enough that she could feel the heat on her neck and smell the beer on his breath.

When Lucy turned her head, he was gone.

CHAPTER 7

Edward One wasn't happy to find Roger lying on the floor, sobbing. After numerous curses and maledictions, he stuck a needle into Roger's neck and unclasped his limp body from the table. Lucy was barely awake, so when Edward righted the table and pushed it out of her view, everything appeared hazy. Multiple Edwards spun in a circle before her eyes. For a flash of time, Lucy swore that she could see her father's face in the middle, the sight jarred her to attention. Her energy was depleted to the point that lifting her head seemed out of the realm of possibility, but she gave it the ol' college try.

Edward left the room for a time, then returned with a tool box. Lucy could only vaguely see the man as he worked, but the sounds told her enough. He was drilling a hole. He grunted and cursed, then left again. Lucy wanted to say something to him; to ask for water, but she couldn't get the words to come out.

A familiar voice behind her spoke then.

"You're going to die here. Just accept it and move on," he said.

The voice, with its cocky drawl, was unmistakable. Todd had returned, dashing Lucy's hopes that her hallucinations had subsided.

Don't talk to him. Ignore him.

"You can't ignore me. I'm back, baby! You know you missed me."

Lucy nearly shouted out, but just as she drew in a breath, she heard the sound. Edward had returned, and though Lucy couldn't see him well, she knew that he was hovering near Roger drilling a hole in the wall. Again, he grunted, cursed, and left.

Afraid that Todd would continue to berate her, Lucy attempted humming to herself. Her tune was muffled and cracked as if split by a chisel. Another sound now, far off this time. She stopped her humming and tried to perk her ears. It started softly, but grew steadily louder. Lucy knew she had heard the sound before, but she strained to place it. Once it had gotten close enough, she knew. Chains. Edward was dragging chains.

When he entered the room, the sound was deafening. Lucy couldn't help but wonder where Edward was able to find heavy chain in an office building. He certainly wasn't gone long enough to go to a hardware store. *Or was he?* Could she even trust her sense of time anymore?

When Edward dropped the chain to the ground, the sound was so loud that Lucy immediately closed her eyes tight and felt an intense reverberation on her scalp. When the agony subsided, she found that it felt a little better with her eyes closed. Given that she couldn't see anything but blurry blobs anyway, she decided to keep her blindness.

The noises didn't let up, the banging of the chains eventually replaced by the loud, stinging sound of a saw blade cutting through metal. Every sound bounced back and forth in the room causing an evil, industrial cacophony that massacred her ears.

Finally, the noise ceased.

Lucy could still hear the ringing in her head, and she didn't know if it would ever go away. When she heard the rustling next to her, she dared to crack her eyelids a bit. Edward was dragging Roger. Lucy tried to speak. With great effort she tried to say, "What are you doing to him?" What came out was more akin to a baby's gurgle than real words.

Roger was propped up against the left wall, and a few loud bangs later, Edward finished his task. Just within her distorted peripheral vision, she could see Edward slide Roger's table out of the room before closing the door and collapsing into his usual spot against the curtain, his previous pile of ash and rubbish still right where he had left it. He pulled his cigarette pack from the front pocket of his long-sleeved shirt. He had rolled up the cuffs, but there were still splotches of sweat stippled haphazardly across his torso.

He pulled the matches from their hiding spot in the cellophane, lit a cigarette, then let out the sigh of a man who has just finished a hard day's work. Lucy doubted that Edward was required to exert himself often, with the possible exception of a racquetball game, or whatever rich people did with their leisure time.

It wasn't until his second cigarette that Edward looked up at her. His solemn expression immediately morphed into one of genuine concern. The shift was shockingly orthodox.

"Shit. You look terrible. How long have you been like this?" he asked.

She moved her lips slightly, but said nothing.

"Hold on," he said, and picked up the jug of water. He held it near her mouth and poured slowly. At first, the liquid choked her, but then she was able to swallow deeply. He kept pouring, and she wasn't about to stop drinking. She must have gotten half a gallon of water in her belly before saying, "Food."

Edward opened a protein bar and fed it to her. Then another. Halfway through her third, she felt sick to her stomach and tilted her face away.

After chewing, she said, "Thanks."

"Sure. Of course. I can't believe you got that close. You could have died."

Lucy's eyes widened in disbelief.

Of course I could have died, you sick fuck!

Yet she kept quiet. Edward sat back down on the floor and lit another cigarette. She was feeling a little better, but it would take some time for her to recover. All she wanted now was more rest.

Sleep came the moment Lucy closed her eyes.

Lucy dreamed of her father. His imposing figure appearing even larger than reality would have shown. The lesson of the day was survival, as it was every day. This was the time that he had sent her into the woods alone. He handed her the knife, larger than she remembered, and a small canteen. Empty. He would meet her on the other side of the forest in three days.

She was twelve years old.

Roger's voice woke her, and she could feel the sweat beading on her brow. Precious, wasted water. She often thought of that weekend in the woods – both in memories and her dreams. The day her father left her behind, driving away in his truck without looking back, was the apex of fear at that point in her short life. She had been scared many times since then, but she always had the one thing that she didn't have now. Tools to get the job done. Now she was helpless, which was far worse than fear. She could *use* fear. While helpless, she could only be used.

"Look." Roger had said several times.

The curtains were open, though not quite all the way, as if Edward didn't have – or feel like taking – the time to fully draw them. Still, the majority of the office was visible, as was the woman inside, sitting across the desk from Edward. Lucy had not seen the woman before, and she looked uneasy, but Edward had a smile on his face. He appeared subtly demented, sat upright at the edge of his chair.

"Have they said anything?" Lucy asked.

"Yeah. I think she's a hooker. Tammy–no, Tonya, but they've been quiet for a long time. He offered her two grand, but I don't know what for. Something about an email he sent her."

Lucy was instantly intrigued, her excitement made her realize just how much the water and food had restored her. The look of unease that Lucy got from the woman was now, obviously, a look of indecision. Feeling a little ashamed, Lucy could not wait to find out what the woman was being asked.

The two of them had eyes locked, the woman's lips quivering, while Edward's smile remained immovable.

Then the woman spoke, "Three."

"Deal," Edward said, immediately standing up and removing his suit jacket. After laying it on the desk, he reached down into the bottom right drawer of his desk and removed a shiny wooden box, placing it down delicately in front of the woman.

"What, here?" she asked.

"Of course. The doors are locked, and as you could see when you came up here, there will be no one to interrupt us."

"Cash up front."

He reached into his pocket and grabbed a wad of money, handing it to her without counting.

"This is three thousand?"

"Sure."

"You knew that's what I would ask for?"

"Some things are just predictable. Take off your clothes. Leave your panties and bra on for now." He said the words with cold, vaporous inflection. He removed his tie, then his shirt, taking his time over the buttons. His abs were even tighter than usual, leading Lucy to think that he had probably worked out recently. She hated herself for noticing such a thing.

Edward opened the mystery box as if it were the lost ark, but when the lid was open, there was no doom awaiting him there. Just a whip. He pulled out a black and red, full-sized bull whip, letting the leather crimp and creak in his hands. Holding the handle, he let the length of it fall to the floor. Lucy could see from here that Edward's knuckles were white as he gripped the leather.

The look of shock on the woman's face was telling as she stood mostly naked in semi-transparent mesh undergarments.

"You did read the email, yes?"

"Yeah," she said, "I just didn't know it was going to be that big. How much is this going to hurt?"

"It's going to sting. Probably a lot. Leave marks."

The woman began to gather up her clothes. "No. I can't. I just can't. Sorry. You can keep your..."

Before she could finish. Edward reached in his pocket and threw out another banded pile of money. As the cash bounced across the floor, he said, "Three more. Double."

The woman's eyes changed; the money taking over her sensibilities. She dropped her clothes and snatched up the cash like it was a magical ring.

"Where do you want me?" she said.

"Put your hands on my desk. Close your eyes. It'll be over before you know it."

"Ok," the woman said, as she assumed the position, "Just, please, try not to leave any scars."

As soon as her hands touched the mahogany, the whip was in the air and sailing toward her bare flesh. As it cracked in a thunderous pop, leaving a diagonal red gash across her skin, he said, "No promises."

The woman's body collapsed onto the floor, and she looked to be screaming, but no sound was made. Her eyes were shocked glass, twitching. Her mind must have still been clouded with the promise of riches as she tried to get back to her feet. Edward smiled, laughed, and let the whip fly again. He crossed his previous mark, leaving a bloody "X" on her previously unblemished backside. The blood was pooling, dripping.

She found her voice. "Stop! Enough!" She was screaming between the words. "I'm finished. Keep...keep your fucking money."

As she grabbed for her clothes, Edward lifted the whip up high and brought it down on her a third time, creating a perfect star shape that she would carry with her forever. She fell to the floor, and lay there flat. Crying. "Please," was all she could say.

"I'm sorry," he said. "Forgive me. I can get carried away. Please take your money, you are free to go." He curled the whip back up and, still holding it, sat on the edge of the desk. He watched her gather up her clothes and put them on, wincing as the delicate fabric of her blouse pressed lightly against the fresh meat blooming from her back. The woman didn't bother with her shoes, or a good-bye. Her walk was at a defeated, agonizing pace. Still, she was able to glance down at the cash in her hand, and even in pain, Lucy could see a slight uptick in the corner of her mouth.

The whip flew out into the space between them so quickly that by the time Lucy and Roger gasped in unison, the leather had already wrapped around the woman's neck three times and stuck. Edward grabbed the handle with both hands and yanked back in a sudden jerk. The woman's neck cracked, the look on her face was of complete bewilderment. She was done. She had endured and she was free to walk away. Wasn't she?

She fell back onto her ass. Her head flopped to the side. The rolls of cash dropped from her hands and her body slumped.

Is she dead?

She certainly wasn't moving.

"Is she dead?" Roger asked.

Lucy chose to watch silently instead of answer.

Holding the handle of the whip, he approached the woman's body and wrapped the length of it around her neck a couple more times, before standing up and moving toward the door. He dragged her, limp and bloody, to the entrance of the office with his makeshift leash.

He pulled her through and closed the door; leaving Lucy and Roger alone again. It was completely quiet. No sign that anyone had heard a thing.

"What do we do?" Roger asked.

Lucy didn't have an answer, so she let the question float in the air looking for a home.

She had been watching the sharks swim for longer than was probably healthy, counting each lap. She had named the big one Humphrey. It was a silly name for a fucked-up fish. Lucy still got the willies from watching the sharks, especially Humphrey, but anything was better than the alternative. She simply could not think about what she had just seen. So, she counted laps.

58.

Was that girl really dead?

59.

Maybe it just looked worse than it was or maybe it was all an act.

60.

Do you really think a man willing to tie two people up in a hidden room would worry too much about killing a prostitute, Lucinda?

Enough!

"Are you ok, Roger?"

"No, I'm not ok. Things are not ok."

"I know, but we have to think clearly. He will be back soon, I am sure of it. We have to try and reason with him, because right now, our voices are our only weapon."

"Whatever. We're stuck here."

She motioned with her chin to the chain that Roger was now tied to. It was secured to a large bolt in the wall, and his hands were bound tight. "How far can you move with that thing?"

"A couple feet, that's it."

"Do you think you could take him?"

"No, I can't even swing my arms, and my legs feel like Jell-O."

"Ok. What can you see?" she asked. "Behind me, I mean."

"Just a few shelves. A couple boxes. Nothing interesting. They are on the wall right next to the double doors."

"Double doors?"

"Yeah. As in two," he said.

"Got it."

"What are you planning to do, lady?"

Before she could tell him that she didn't have a plan yet, Lucy heard the door swing open. Edward walked past and looked through the glass.

"Can we get some water?" Roger asked.

"No. Just shut up for a minute," Edward snapped.

When Edward's arms stopped shaking and fell limp to his sides, Lucy knew what was coming. "Get ready," she said.

"For what?" asked Roger.

"Edward Two is coming."

They couldn't take their eyes off him, even though he wasn't moving. The sharks ticked time by as they swam, the air grew stale as it filled with anticipation. Despite keeping a wary vigil, they both jumped when Edward turned around.

"I'm sorry," he said. "I can't imagine what you might think of me."

Lucy stayed silent, but Roger couldn't hold back. "You killed that girl! With a fucking whip for Christ sake. What the fuck is wrong with you?! What are you going to do with us?"

Edward's eyes widened, still black as night, but with a slight glint of orange. He stumbled over to Roger, and knelt before him – just out of reach.

"I've let you down. I know you expect so much more from me, Father. I will make it up to the family. I promise I will."

"Fuck off! I'm not your daddy. Snap out of it!"

"Dad, please don't say that. Don't forsake me. I'll do better. I...I will make you proud, if you just give me another chance."

"He doesn't really hear you," Lucy said. "This part of him only lives in his own piece of reality. To him, you are just the disapproving father. When he changes back, I don't think he will even remember what he said."

"This is so messed up," said Roger.

Edward was crying and bowing his head, his body convulsing, shoulders shaking.

"Edward, why did you kill that woman?" Lucy asked, timidly. He looked over to her, drying his eyes.

"She was bad, Momma."

"Did she deserve to die?"

"They all deserve to die," he answered.

How can I get through to him?

"What did you do with her, Edward?" Lucy asked.

"It doesn't matter. I can handle it. You have never had any faith in me!"

He stood and began to pace the room. He was seething, his hands clenched tight. Lucy didn't know if it was anger at her, or frustration built through misunderstanding, but she dared not say another word to him. His hinges were already off; one small gust of wind would send the door of his temper soaring off into nothing.

Lucy glanced at Roger and gave him a look that she hoped said, "Ok, we can't say anything else."

It didn't.

"You get your rocks off killing girls?" asked Roger, "Why don't you untie me and we'll see who hurts who?"

Edward stopped his pacing but made no move at all toward Roger. Instead, he knelt in front of Lucy, looking up into her eyes. His face was sad and looked like he had walked a thousand miles to her feet.

"I will protect you and we will be a real family again. Dad can't stop it. I will stop him."

Should I tell him I'm not his mother? Why? What would be the point?

He stood again, never taking his eyes from her. He leaned in and kissed her mouth. Lucy didn't bother to fight it. There was no chance for her. His lips lingered on hers for a few moments longer than a son would normally kiss his mother, and when he was finished, Edward turned to look at Roger. Lucy could see bubbling hatred in the black holes of his eyes.

"I don't need protecting," she said.

"You always say that."

Edward backed away and drew the curtain, then walked to the door. Lucy heard it open seconds before the light shifted to fluorescent.

From behind her, he repeated, "You always say that, but you're wrong."

CHAPTER 8

Lucy knew that something was amiss the moment her brain kicked back on. Her arms were tingling all over, and her legs were bent. She was no longer tied to the table, but lay on the frigid floor. When she cracked her eyes, the red curtain was there to greet her.

Her body was so sore and rigid that she had a hard time moving, but she slowly managed to scoot her arm across the floor and up to her face, finding her wrist covered in caked blood, but restraints gone. After saying a tiny prayer, she attempted to wiggle her fingers and found that she could still use her hand.

She stretched out her arm to fight the atrophy, and as her hand extended outward, her fingertips grazed the bottom of the curtain. She felt the fabric between her thumb and forefinger.

Velvet, just as she had thought.

Gradually, she extended each extremity, trying not to work too hard, too fast. She was aware of the dangers of sudden movement after a long period of stillness; blood clots being the most prevalent.

Fool, have you not considered why you are down here in the first place?

This couldn't be a rescue. Who would rescue her then leave her on the floor? Maybe the part of Edward she had first met in the store finally felt guilty and had decided to let her go.

She sat up slowly, immediately realizing that Roger was not in the room. The chains that had bound him were coiled on the floor. Lucy thought to call out, then thought better of it.

It took her a long time to notice the card. It was folded in half, and had the word "Mom" printed messily on the side facing her. Instinctively, she shied away from the card, trying to pretend that she hadn't seen it. She wasn't ready for whatever fucked up horror show that was going to lead to; not just yet anyway.

Lucy scooted past the card, decimating the pile of ash with her ass as she did so. The jug of water was still there, as were the protein bars, though she was sure there wasn't as much left as there had been before. Taking no time to consider, she drank the remainder of the water.

It wasn't until her first swallow that she felt the collar wrapped around her neck. Choosing to ignore that mystery too, she instead downed the last three protein bars from the box, then leaned against the curtained wall.

Breathing heavily, her eye caught the card in its peripheral. She was going to have to face it, whatever it turned out to be. She took a deep breath and let it out slowly.

No daughter of mine is just going to die in the woods. I taught you better than that. Now take a step, how else are you going to get anywhere?

"This is much darker than the woods, Dad." she whispered to herself as she snatched up the card. The handwriting looked like someone with an unsteady hand trying to print as clearly as possible.

Your presence is requested in the dining room.
The collar you wear is electrified and will kill you.
Do not try to escape, follow every instruction
to continue living.

Your Loving Son,
Edward

She immediately grabbed for the collar, trying to find a way to remove it, but there was a lock resting at the back of her neck. She pulled at the thick leather that pressed against her neck but there was no give.

How long ago did he put this on me and where the hell is the dining room?

Standing was harder than it had ever been in her life. Every exertion of muscle or tendon needed stern force, and Lucy was convinced that there was no way she would be able to take a step if she were even able to get upright.

But, stand she did, and even though the first step threatened to throw her back to the floor, she held in place; albeit at a wobble. A few more steps, and she was able to balance herself on the metal table to catch her breath. From there, she could see the double doors, large and wooden, as well as the shelves that Roger had spoken of. She rummaged through what was there, but didn't find anything to use as a weapon, or any other kind of tool.

The dining room.

She didn't know where it was, but she knew it had to be on the other side of the door. Slowly, she turned the knob and pushed the door forward; sliding her feet across the floor inch by inch. Lucy found herself in a hallway, but not one that she would have expected in an office building. There were baseboards painted green, papered walls, a small shelf with a vase filled with silk flowers, and vinyl tiling on the floor. The hallway seemed more like a home than an office.

There was a wall to her right, so Lucy had no choice but to head left. The new hallway had no lights on, but just ahead there was a room on the right with an open door. Light from the room illuminated her path just enough. Bracing herself as best she could on the wall, she dragged her body down to the new room.

Inside there was nothing save the table to which Roger had once been tied, a pile of fancy clothes with another note, and a pile of discarded clothes that were unmistakably Roger's. Bending down was a pain, but she was able to fetch the note. It contained only one word: "Change".

Below the note was a blue cocktail dress folded neatly on the floor with underwear folded on top. She didn't want to play this game. He held all the cards and it sickened her. Still, another part of her was desperate to get out of the clothes she was in. They were most likely over a week old, covered with piss and sweat stains; a smell that ripened with age.

She took her shirt off and dropped it near Roger's things. Just as she was about to remove her bra and change she felt a gut punch. Even in this empty room, she didn't want to reveal herself. This was Edward's domain, and whether he was in the room or not, Lucy could feel his presence.

Follow every instruction to continue living.

Crystal clear.

Removing her bra was a momentary lapse into heaven for her, even with the discomfort she felt with her surroundings. It felt amazing to be free of the grimy old things that had covered her skin. The bra that Edward had left her was lewd, and she had not worn anything like it in many years. It was made of mesh and she could see right through it, making her feel like a whore. At a younger age, she would have had no problem with such revealing lingerie, but Todd had grown to hate it on her, demanding that she wear something more sensible. He liked it in the early days, but soon decided that it was improper for her to go out in public wearing "that filth". He would lift her shirt and check nearly every time she left the house. Even after Todd was gone, she never wore sexy lingerie again, feeling that the window of opportunity for such things had closed on her.

After she removed the remainder of her clothes and put on the new matching underwear, her transformation into a whore was complete. Edward's whore.

His whore mom.

She couldn't get the dress on quick enough. She tried to pull up the zipper on the back, but it snagged the fabric and she couldn't budge it further. Try as she might, she was going to have to continue down the hall in a dress that was falling off her shoulders and underwear that itched like the dickens.

Begrudgingly, Lucy made her way further down the hallway, coming to a right corner several dozen hard fought steps later. In front of her was another door, this one closed. She approached it carefully, trying not to make much noise, but failing as her feet dragged across the ground. She put her ear to the wood but couldn't hear anything. Her dress had already fallen from her shoulders, leaving her chest exposed. She pulled it back on the best she could and opened the door.

She had found the dining room. An exceptionally long table lined with a dozen high backed chairs dominated the space, candelabras positioned around the room, as well as in the center of the table, and flowering plants in expensive vases on intricately carved stands. Lucy felt as if she were meeting Count Dracula for dinner, until she approached the table and could see one of the candelabras better. It wasn't flame coming from the candles but small light bulbs made to look like flickering fire. The dripping wax was a mere illusion and a closer inspection proved the plants fake as well.

What is all this?

Roger was sitting on the far end of the table. Not at the head, but one seat to its left. He pointed toward her but said nothing. It took a moment for Lucy to see what he was motioning to, but then she found the card on the table, once again marked "Mom".

She took the steps to the table and found that her muscles were finally beginning to loosen. Again, she wanted to turn her back on the note. She wanted to go back to her room, turn on the orange light, and strap herself back to the table.

Her hands seemed to understand the thought as foolish before her mind did, she was looking down at the note before she realized they were even moving.

Sit across from Dad. He is not
happy. I'm afraid he may grow
angry. Remember your collar.

Love,
Edward

Lucy nearly ripped the note in half, but was too afraid that it might be breaking a rule. She couldn't let petty feelings end in electrocution. Step by step, she made her way to the end of the table, opposite Roger. She had to stop once to catch her breath, but was feeling better overall. The air in the dining room was easier to breathe.

After sitting in her chair, she looked over at Roger who was trying to avert his eyes from her.

"How long have you been in here?" she asked.

"I don't know. Maybe fifteen minutes."

"Have you seen him?"

"No," he answered, dismissively.

Roger clearly didn't want to talk and still couldn't look at her. She could only imagine what any notes meant for him might have said.

Just ask him.

The plate in front of her was intricately painted in blue scroll work, the silverware appeared sterling, and the linen napkin was nice enough to make her think twice about touching it, let alone using it to wipe food off her face.

Just ask him.

Fine.

"Did you get a note?"

"Yeah."

"What did it say?"

"I don't want to talk about it," he said, with inflection that put a definitive end to the conversation.

Before she could hassle him further, a swinging door opened wide and Edward stepped through, the door whooshing wide, a little less with each pass. In his hands, Edward carried two silver trays. He set one down in front of each of them. There was nothing on the trays besides another note card.

"Enjoy your appetizers. Please, only eat from your own tray. I will be back soon to enjoy dinner with you." He stood looking at them as they both stared back at him, and smiled. "It is so nice to be sitting down together for dinner. We so rarely get the chance anymore. Dad, I hope everything is to your satisfaction."

Roger's eyes went wide as he suddenly realized that Edward was expecting a response.

"Um. Yeah, sure. It's nice."

"Okay, Dad, but can I get you anything to calm you down? I want you to be happy."

"I'm fine. I guess," Roger stated.

"Very well then. Enjoy your first course." Then, he walked out again, the door swinging wildly.

The two dinner guests looked at their respective note cards, then back at each other. Neither made an immediate move to read theirs. Lucy felt as if she was now in some sort of competition with her roommate on top of everything else.

"Look," she said, "This may go a lot better if we each knew what the other was having to deal with."

"I can't tell you. I'm sorry – for all of it."

Roger grabbed his card from the tray and set it down on his plate, as if it were an actual morsel of food to be admired and savored. He looked at Lucy one more time, but so quickly it was barely perceptible, then picked up and read his card. His already somber expression changed subtly, and not for the better.

Fearing that pushing him into talking more may lead to dire consequences, Lucy grabbed her own card and flipped it over.

Daddy is very angry tonight.
You must make him angrier by
nagging him. Do it well, or you'll
be in for a shock.

Edward

Nag him?

Was she supposed to ask him more about his notes? What was she to nag him about?

Thinking it over, Lucy stared into the empty glass on the table in front of her, wishing to hell it was filled to the brim with merlot. Any kind would do, even the cheap stuff from a box. She imagined how divine the wine would taste on her tongue, how much better it would feel in her mind minutes later.

She was jostled from her fantasy when the door swung open again. Watching the door swing back and forth made her eyes cross, so she looked away. This time, Edward didn't carry anything. He pulled the head chair out from under the table, then made a noisy show of scooting himself back in.

"I hope dinner is going well so far. I do apologize for my tardiness. Thank you, Father, for letting me sit at the head of the table. You know how I like to feel important."

"Yeah. No problem," Roger answered.

"Mother, I trust you had a good day."

Lucy was at a loss. She could understand that this was supposed to be a meal with Edward's family, but she didn't know how to proceed — especially knowing that her life depended on getting it right. *Nag him*, the note had said. *Nag him*.

Nag him.

"My day would have been a lot better if I could have counted on your father," she said, praying that she was making the right choice.

"Oh, what is it now!" Roger shouted.

The amplitude of his response startled her, but Edward's face showed that they were on the right track.

He was scared.

Like a child presented with the idea of death for the first time, Edward cowered back in his chair and sucked on his lower lip. Lucy thought over her next words. Acting had never been one of her strengths, and she was having a hard time thinking on her toes.

"I've asked...I've asked you a hundred times to..."

"Just shut your mouth," Roger interrupted, though he looked down at his plate as he spoke. "No one here wants to listen to your bullshit."

"Dad, please. Mom works very hard," Edward spoke in a small voice.

"You think I don't work?!"

"I know you do, Father. I just want us to get along. I am going to check on dinner. Please. Just love each other."

Edward rolled his body out of the chair, grabbed the two silver platters, and disappeared behind the swinging door once more. Lucy reached up to touch her collar, as if checking it would prevent her from electrocution. When she looked up, she saw that Roger was checking his too.

"Do you think we did it right?" she asked.

"It isn't over yet," is all Roger had to say.

Minutes passed in silence. Lucy rocked from side to side in her chair, a habit she formed when she was a small child. Her nervous movements used to drive her father up the wall. He used to tell her that if she couldn't keep her body still, then she would never be able to still her mind either. He had been right about that.

As if he had heard her thoughts, her father appeared; taking a step from the darkest corner of the room and walking towards the dining table. He didn't speak, but his look was of disgust. Why had he come? She pulled her dress up, embarrassed to have her father see her this way. He sat at the other end of the table, on the same side as Roger. As she looked at her father, movement caught her eye. Todd was there too, sitting across from her father. He was laughing, but no sound emanated from his lips.

The sight of them made her ill. Roger did not see them; of course not. They were her hallucinations, and hers alone. But she was feeling better, wasn't she? Why were they here?

When Edward returned, he carried another platter, though this one had a massive roast turkey to weigh it down. In a flash, the thought of real food lifted Lucy's spirits, but when Edward lowered the new platter to the table, her hopes were just as dramatically dashed.

It wasn't real.

The turkey was plastic and not even a convincing replica. The bed of lettuce that it sat upon was made from paper. Edward left to bring back a large bowl filled with fake mashed potatoes, a plate covered in ersatz corn-on-the-cob, and an empty bottle of wine – which, perhaps, mocked her the most.

Roger looked angry. Very angry. Lucy thought that he would fly off the handle and get himself killed, but he seemed to just sit in his fury, letting it pool around him. Edward appeared quite satisfied while he looked at them in hopeful anticipation.

"Doesn't this just look amazing?" he said, more upbeat than he had been when he left. "Mom sure outdid herself this time, huh, Dad?"

Her father sighed and said softly, "Watch out."

Roger seethed, breathing in deeply and quickly. His face was turning red yet still he said nothing. Lucy got the idea that he was building to something – maybe psyching himself up for an attack. Would he try? She wondered if he could get to Edward and shut him down before the collar shocked him to death. She didn't even know how the collar was supposed to work, but she assumed Edward had some kind of control, probably on his person. She didn't want to die, but maybe this really was their best chance.

She looked over at Roger, quietly willing him to look in her direction. When he finally did, he had a fury in his eyes so fiery it glowed, she gave him a slight nod.

Go for it. Get him.

If this had been a cartoon, steam would be blowing out of Roger's ears. He pivoted his body, nearly standing, but then retreating again. Over and over he did this, until the inevitable explosion finally came.

"This dinner is fucking unacceptable!" he screamed, standing. "Your cooking has never been any good." He was yelling and looking directly at Lucy. When he reached down, grabbed the tray and threw it across the room, she felt confusion. How was this going to help them escape? Was it just a distraction?

As Roger grabbed her by the collar and pulled her across the table, Lucy could still only think that any moment he would make his move on Edward. Any second, they would tackle their captor to the ground and fight for their freedom.

The first punch killed those thoughts. The second made it difficult for her to breathe. Roger's fists slammed into her mouth. Her nose. Into her left eye. The pain was maddening and she couldn't get a clear enough thought in her head to react. She should fight back, but how to move with a mouth full of blood, and a nose that seems to have ceased breathing.

Her ex-husband's laughter was perfectly audible now.

Edward's words were distant and hazy.

"No, Father!"

"Stop, Dad!"

"She did the best she could!"

The hitting stopped and a blurry Roger backed away from the table. Lucy slowly tried to roll her body over. Perhaps she could still get away if she could just find her footing. If she could just see the path of escape.

The best she accomplished was to sink back off the table and into her chair. Her eyes threatened to black out; but either her stubbornness or her physiognomy prevented her from fully passing out. Still, she couldn't move any further, blood flowing freely from her face down to her exposed chest, above the ill-fitting dress that had bunched around her waist. "Finish," Edward said, in a much deeper voice than he had so far used that night. It was a forceful tone that Lucy heard clear as a bell.

Roger heard it too.

He walked around the back of Edward, and for a blink, even now, Lucy had a hope that this was the moment that Roger would make his move on their host - their 'son' - but he passed Edward by and stood before Lucy.

"You...you...you're a constant...disappointment," he said to Lucy, before slamming his fist into her once more.

Her eyes went dark, her head a noxious cloud. He hit her one final time, and just before Lucy lost consciousness; she heard a few final words.

"No, Daddy, stop hurting her!"

CHAPTER 9

Roger was crying.

The hard, cold metal beneath her told Lucy she was back on her table. There wasn't a sufficient descriptor for her pain. She had taken beatings in her life. Once from an older girl in freshman year of high school. A whole bunch more at Todd's hands.

This pain was on another level. She wasn't hurt; she was damaged.

When she tried to open her eyes, only her right eye cracked wide. Her left eye sent an electric shock through her head that Lucy was sure would rival anything that damn collar could have caused. She didn't need a mirror to know that her eye was shades of purple and black.

Roger hadn't noticed that she had woken and was still a blubbering mess. The man that beat her was crying about it. History was repeating itself yet again.

She didn't think her nose was broken, so she counted that as a blessing, but the blood caked over her mouth cracked apart as she used her tongue to check her teeth. Her lower jaw was missing a bicuspid on the left side, and the next molar over was very loose.

Still, *Roger* was the one crying.

"Get it together," she said, straining.

His gurgling, snotty noise finally stopped. Lucy was sure that the beating Roger had given her was not of his own design, but she couldn't help but hate the man a little.

"Oh, thank God, you're awake!"

"Praise Him and all that jazz. How long have I been out?"

"I don't know. A long time. He hasn't come back in since he brought us back, and he didn't open the curtains. I haven't heard anything on the intercom either."

His words felt like boulders on her skull, though Lucy doubted he was speaking much louder than a whisper. He sniffled repeatedly, which only drove Lucy crazy. *Wasn't she the one entitled to tears?*

Lucy felt like Roger was stealing her sadness away and making it his, even though he was the cause.

"Roger, you are going to have to knock it off. Okay? It's time to move on."

It was a harsh sentiment that came from pure exhaustion. Lucy suddenly realized a very important thing; her fear wasn't there anymore. Well, not so prominently anyway. Roger must have beat it all out, leaving only her father's daughter. She had forgotten herself as the days passed but she now had a renewed sense of purpose.

She would get out, whatever it took.

"What did your notes say?" she asked.

"Um. The first one said that I was angry. 'You've hit mother before, why not again?' If I didn't play my role, I would be killed with electricity."

"And the next?"

"'You had a bad day and Mom isn't making it better. Will you let her talk to you like that?' I didn't know what the fuck to do until you said that shit about being able to count on me. So, I got angry like the note said."

"And why wouldn't you tell me that when I sat down?" Lucy asked.

"Because, there was a post script. 'Keep it a secret or die before dinner.'"

Lucy nodded her head, but only once, the pain was too intense.

"I'm sorry you had to go through that," she said. She wasn't sorry, but she needed to get a hold of the situation in any way that she could, and holding onto anger was never going to help.

Starting to cry again, Roger said, "Please don't apologize to me. I'm the one who is sorry. I don't know how I could have done that to you. I'm not that kind of guy. I've never..."

"Hush! Did you want to die? No. If I was going to die, I'd beat the shit out of you too. Like I said, it's time to move on."

This pain is nothing.

"Okay," Roger said.

"You got another note, didn't you?"

"Yes. It just said," he said, choking back tears, "It said, 'Beat her until she sleeps'."

That was that. He didn't have a choice. Lucy shut her eyes again, a need for rest overtaking her. She would wake with purpose.

"What do we do now?" Roger asked.

"We wait."

She awoke to open curtains; it felt like they had been closed for days. Edward was at his desk, shuffling through a large stack of papers, and Bonnie was in the chair across from him, shuffling through another stack on her lap.

"Were you awake when he came in?" she asked.

"Yeah. He cleaned your face with a washcloth and gave you water," Roger answered, "You drank a bit, but not much. He didn't say anything to me at all."

"He wouldn't. *That* Edward sees you as his enemy. The father that he never stood up to. Never protected his mother from. You need to watch yourself. Don't let your guard down."

Lucy let that sink in for him as she assessed her own body. It was broken, same as it ever was. She couldn't stand another day of waiting for doom to fall. She had to do something, and right now, all she had was her voice.

"Tell me some more about your life, Roger."

"There isn't much to tell."

"I don't care about the minutia of it all, Roger. Tell me something juicy. Help me pass the day with a little intrigue. It's the least you can do for smashing my face in," Lucy said, tilting her head and smiling a painful smile.

"Let me think about it," he said.

"Sure, but it isn't like I have all the time in the world here, Roger."

She giggled, and it made her soul hurt. Laughter was a commodity swiftly vanishing into the dust. The orange light was sucking it all up and refusing to spit it back out.

"Okay. I cheated on my wife for almost a year. Nearly left her. Then I found out that the woman I was seeing was married too. She never had plans of leaving her husband and I was just a fling. I felt guilty, told my wife, then she left me."

"Did you ever get remarried?"

"No. I'm done with all of that."

Lucy could tell by the inflection in his voice that Roger's story was the only one he had. His entire life probably revolved around that mistake. It probably always would. Lucy had many stories to tell, but there was only one that mattered. *Should she let it out?* She would probably never have a life again anyway. How to tell?

Be blunt. Fuck it, right?

"I killed my husband. Well, technically I let him die. Same thing really."

Roger looked up at her, having previously kept to staring fixedly into the floor. His eyes asked for more information, but he didn't have the energy for words.

"We were together for a long time. He wasn't a nice man. Todd was his name," Lucy said, remembering as she spoke. "One night he came home drunk. He usually did. He hit me for not having dinner ready for him. It was after one in the morning, but I don't think he put that together in his drunk head.

"He tried to hit me again when he saw that I didn't flinch the first time. I had grown too used to his violence. I moved out of the way and he sort of fell into me. I let his body fall and his head knocked against the corner of our dining table. It was solid — an antique.

"His body hit the floor so hard that one of the tiles cracked. I remember being more upset about that tile than the hurt he had put on me. That crack filled up with blood, and I guess that was when I knew there was a problem. He rolled over and reached up to me. He gurgled for help. I just let him lie there, watching the puddle grow." Lucy paused a moment, remembering how much blood there was. "I could have helped, called someone, stopped the bleeding. But I let him die. After, I poured some of the whiskey I had hidden from him and had myself a drink."

"Jesus," Roger said. "Why are you telling me this?"

"Because this may be my last chance. I never told anyone. The police just believed he fell down drunk and died while I was sleeping. They just let it go."

"Look. Lady, from now on, let's just keep quiet, ok? I don't need this. You can talk to me again when you have a brilliant plan to get us out of here."

Lucy didn't blame him and hadn't expected much more from the man. She simply had to say it out loud, didn't matter to whom. Now, it was out there in the ether, and there was nothing she could do to get it back.

She felt light, feathery, and thirsty.

Later, Edward paid them a visit. His concern for Lucy was plastered on his face, as was his disdain for Roger. He used a washcloth on her face and chest again, the cool water stinging the cracks in her flesh. She was still unable to open her left eye.

"I am so sorry that he did this to you," Edward said as he closed the curtain and changed the light. The brightness of the fluorescent bulb was unwelcomed by Lucy, its brightness like a blade to her eyes. "I should have stopped him."

"Well, you always were a disappointing little shit," she said, shocking even herself. She had no idea where the words came from, they flew against everything that she had planned to say. She had wanted to play along until opportunity for escape arose but now she threatened any progress she had made on that front.

Edward looked hurt, and pulled the wash rag from her skin. "I...I know. I'm trying to fix it, Mother."

"Fix it faster," Lucy said.

She didn't know what was happening to her. One moment she was quivering and giving up, the next her resolve was unbreakable. Now, she had somehow turned into an unthinking bitch. From moment to moment she either had a plan, or not. Her thoughts were scattered and she couldn't find their center. She wanted to help Edward, just as she wanted to kill him.

Before any further words were spoken, the intercom suddenly flared up. It was Bonnie's voice through Edward's office com. "Mr. Wolcroft, you have a visitor. He doesn't believe that you aren't in and is refusing to leave."

Edward flew out of the room, and Lucy knew it wasn't just because of his visitor. She had hurt him. She may have made a little crack in that fucked up brain of his. Maybe she was thinking more clearly than she gave herself credit, or she was delusional. It was so hard to tell anymore.

Just a few minutes later, Edward was rushing into his office by the side entrance and sitting at his desk. He pulled his chair up so far that his midriff must have been squished against the desk's edge. He sat himself upright, Lucy could see him try and create the appropriate persona for the meeting. A buzz came from his com, and Bonnie cleared her throat before saying, "He doesn't seem to want to see reason, sir."

"Send him in."

Edward snatched up the nearest file and began to look through it, a clear ruse. Bonnie burst in and held the door for a tall man in a grey suit. Edward would have business associates trickle in from time to time, but this was a new face for Lucy. The man stood a full foot or more over Bonnie and as he passed her, he made a motion as if tipping a hat, though he wore none.

"Have a seat," Edward said, not looking up from his file.

"I prefer to stand, if it's all the same."

"Suit yourself. I'll be with you in a moment. Let my assistant know if you would like a beverage."

The man stood just a few feet in front of the desk with his hands folded delicately in front of him. His look was stern, yet calm. Lucy could see Edward's leg twitch up and down below the desk.

He is scared of this man.

"While I am sure the production reports from the textiles division circa 2014 are very important," the tall man said, reading the file tab. "I do have pressing business elsewhere. Do you think we could skip the first few steps of this act and let me tell you why I'm here?"

Edward didn't drop the file immediately, a stubborn showing of power, but he did look up at the man. "Mr. Henderson, are sure you wouldn't like to take a seat?" he asked, finally closing the file and laying it on the desk. He folded his hands together atop the file and smiled.

"If it will speed things along, I will sit. And, as I have told you before, it is Agent Henderson."

"My apologies."

"Yes, well, I will get right to it. A woman was found dead. Washed up on the river bank about five minutes from here. Coroner says she was asphyxiated with some sort of cord. Also, said it happened no more than two days ago. We think she was a whore. High end."

"Riveting. What does it have to do with me?" Edward asked, his leg still fidgeting.

"Well we both know that you like the expensive ones, Mr. Wolcroft, and it happening so close to your beautiful building here, I thought why not pop in on my old friend and see if he had heard anything about it."

"No."

"So, you didn't strangle a girl a couple days ago?"

"No. Is that all?"

"I wish. I really do. But my work never seems to be done. I keep coming here, and all you ever respond to my questions is, 'No'. The same answer so many times in a row might lead a man to think another man was lying."

"This big act you put on, making yourself out to be the reincarnation of J. Edgar Hoover – it's bad fiction. So, I will speak more plainly for you. You think I killed a prostitute, and I am telling you I didn't. So, unless you have a warrant of some kind, I'll ask you to please get the hell out of my office. I have work to do," Edward responded.

"Yes, the textile division. Seems imperative. I'll leave you to it, but I'll visit again soon." The man – Agent Henderson – stood and walked to the door. "In case you are concerned for the poor dead whore, let me tell you that with a struggle that comes from strangulation, there's always evidence somewhere. Hair follicles, maybe skin. Who knows, that isn't my job."

He opened the door, and just as it was about to shut, Henderson popped his head back in. "I almost forgot. As I was pulling up, I noticed that your car was being towed from the garage. The truck driver asked me to give you this piece of paper." Henderson dropped a folded paper on the floor, then departed.

Edward immediately hit the button on the com, "Bonnie, get the fuck in here."

She was in the door in a heartbeat, stepping on the paper. She bent down to pick it up and a tear dripped from her lashes.

"It says 'warrant'."

"No shit. They took my car," he said, moving briskly across the office to where Bonnie stood. He slapped her hard across the face, so hard that Bonnie fell to the ground. "I pay you for two things; to suck my cock, and keep people out of here. Don't fail me again."

Bonnie left the office on her knees, probably too scared to stand and face her boss again. Lucy wanted to act shocked, but she found that the feeling didn't come. The only thing she could think about was Henderson. Someone was on to Edward and that was the first good news that had come Lucy's way in a long time. Despite what she had seen lately, Lucy smiled. The blood still caked on her mouth cracked, sending flakes of what had once flowed through her veins to the floor.

Edward paced his office, appearing as just another shark; drifting around with no way out. He shouted incoherently several times, his voice an echo of fear. It made Lucy happy to see him like this, but still a part of her wanted to know more; wanted to dissect his psyche and poke at what she found. That tiny part of her that didn't like to see *anyone* suffer.

In mid stride, Edward stopped in his tracks, his body slack; an automaton whose battery had died. There he remained as the sky darkened. Bonnie did not return, but Lucy wouldn't have expected her to. Maybe she finally got it in her silly head that this wasn't the job for her. When Edward moved again, it was to the side door.

He's coming.

Lucy's mild thrill rapidly dissipated as she realized that there was no predicting how this would affect Edward, or what he might do. Her hands were tight in fists that could not be used; her legs primed for a run that would not come.

It took longer than Lucy expected, but the door eventually opened. Edward closed the curtain, but did not switch the light. Without the ambient light from the glass, the room was horror drenched. The orange glow cast shadows that made no sense to her. Her eyes couldn't adjust properly, and movement in her peripheral startled her repeatedly – turning out to be figments of an imagination that hadn't had reality to steady itself for far too long.

In his hand, Edward carried the same collar that he had used to beat her. Sure, he hadn't used his own hands, but he pulled the strings. She and Roger were his puppets; a Punch and Judy show from Hell.

Edward wasted no time locking the collar back on her neck.

"What do you want now? Am I not bruised enough for you yet?"

Instead of words, Edward raised his hand to silence her. Despite the fury in Lucy, the motion worked.

"Remember your collar, Mother," he said calmly, then began to unclasp her restraints.

Roger, who until now had been as useful as a lawn gnome, suddenly sparked to life.

"Hey! Hey, what are you doing to her? Leave us alone. I don't want to do this again!"

Edward didn't act like he had heard anything.

After he had both of her hands unfastened, he used one of the leather restraints to bind her wrists together. When he was done, there was no give at all for her to try anything. Not that she would anyway, the collar saw to that. She wondered if maybe it was all just a ruse. Maybe the collar wasn't electrified at all. Maybe all she had to do was run as soon as he finished unclasping her feet.

No, Lucinda, don't be stupid. Maybe it is and maybe it isn't, but the price for being wrong is death.

Edward helped her balance herself as her feet touched the floor. When she was able to stand up straight, they were eye to eye. She felt like she was falling into those eyes, scraping and clawing at the edges of the well to his inner self. It had never been like her to think in such a way in normal life, but now every moment seemed like the poetry of adolescents.

He touched her face, and she took a step back, cowering. With his left hand, he reached out and yanked her back to him, gently caressing her cheek with the right. Even his soft touch was a hailstorm on her battered skin.

"I'm so sorry," he said. "I couldn't stop him."

Then he began to cry. Lucy was tired of seeing grown men weep.

He grabbed her tightly around the waist and began to force her to her knees. Fearing what was next, she fought back, damn the collar. But, her body was weak, and he forced her down. Instead of what she feared, he went to the ground beside her, and they kneeled together.

"I want to lie with you again, Mother. Like when I was a baby. I want you to love me like I was innocent. I need to feel your warmth."

She wanted to protest. The tears that ran down his face made him seem pathetic. A man incapable of killing her. Still, she couldn't risk an escape attempt, and laying with him was certainly better than what her mind dreaded.

As he pushed her to the side, her knee slipped, and her head crashed against the floor. Her neck cracked, and her head became as clouds encircling a mountaintop. She rolled over onto her back and shut her eyes, her ears ringing, head thumping. She felt the warmth of another body against her side, and when Edward put his arm around her, Lucy felt like she was suffocating. She could hear him speak, but couldn't make out the words, her ears still on their coffee break.

His hand rested on her sternum and the weight made her aware of how fast her heart was beating. She couldn't take another moment.

"Get off me!" she shouted, trying desperately to turn away from him. "I am not your mother. Just let me go, fucking psychopath!"

Edward gripped her shoulder and pulled her back over easily. He held her down with a single hand. His eyes were on her again, and she couldn't look away. He laid his head down on her, just above her right breast. Her entire torso was heaving with lost breaths and speeding ticks of her heart. He raised his right leg and placed it over her body, so that his thigh was resting atop her middle.

There he lay.

Not a word from his mouth, not a twitch of his limbs.

Lucy's heart slowed, and her breathing normalized. Edward's eyes were closed. She was going to be okay.

I am going to be okay.

This pain is nothing.

This pain is...

Edward's hand pushed outward, and his fingers curled around her breast. Lucy held her breath entirely as he felt her up before stopping and pulling her dress down by the neck. She had never managed to get the zipper up in the back, and the garment gave no resistance to being pulled all the way down to her waist. He bunched the fabric up there, then moved his attention back to her chest.

His hands explored her freely, and Lucy felt the smallest amount of bile build in her throat. His touch was soft, and that made the experience worse. If he was going to take her, she wanted him to do it by force, with power; not with affection. She attempted to push him away with her bound hands, but didn't have the strength for a fight.

He nestled into her like a lover on a rainy night, trying to get as close as possible, drawing warmth from each her flesh. Edward lined his mouth up with her right breast, and gently pulled it toward him so he could suckle her. Fear rushed through her body and into him as he played out his infantile fantasy.

She closed her eyes once more, desperate to think of anything else, to be anywhere but on that floor with him. As her father had taught her, she began to breathe rhythmically. It took her several tries, as the sounds of Edward drawing her nipple inside his mouth grew louder, but she made it back to her forest. The trees were green, and smelled of summer.

This is where I belong. This is where I am.

In the distance, she heard the sound of a zipper, but she focused on the trees.

This is my forest, and no other person can come here but me.

She felt movement against her leg, slapping into her thigh. Edwards breathing grew heavy, but the trees were calling her. Lucy began to walk over to the tree line to begin another journey through to the other side. The bird's song drowned out the far-off sound.

The smell of cedar and pine filled her nose, as the pounding on her thigh rapidly increased, then stopped.

CHAPTER 10

"It is what it is."

"I just wish I could have done something. It makes me so sick," said Roger.

"If you start crying again, I swear I will scream."

Lucy's facade was pure steel, but inside she was the last remnants of a burning tealight, soon to extinguish. Edward had strapped her back to the table without cleaning the disgusting sludge that tarnished her thigh. He *had* been kind enough to replace her dress, zipping it properly – so, small miracles.

He left the collar on, a chafing reminder that more was to come, and also put a collar back on Roger, who had done his best to fight back until Edward threatened Lucy's life if he didn't supplicate. Since then, Roger had been a mess of emotion— the heart on his sleeve so exposed that it slid down across the floor, leaving a trail of bloody tears that wouldn't cease.

Edward had fed them both, and supplied plenty of water. After a nap of indeterminate length, Lucy felt like the shiniest car on a sleazy used lot, her mind was less of a heavy fog, and more a late morning mist. The pain she felt in virtually every area of her head was ever-present, but paled in comparison to her mental state. She could not fathom a way through what had happened to her. Every thought she had of Edward slithering across her body, imbibing her flesh, seemed too much to comprehend, so, she didn't try. Lucy turned from those thoughts, and though they were constantly tapping her on her shoulder, she refused to give them attention.

The red curtain was closed, and she wondered if Edward was on the other side. It was funny how little knowledge she had of her situation, how small her world had become. Behind the curtain was the only thing she had now. All knowledge came from the other side of the glass; and if she didn't have that, she had nothing.

Just rationalize, Lucinda. He left the collars on. That means he will come for you again. The time for waiting for the right moment is over.

"Roger, we have to have a plan."

He was twitching the end of his chain across the ground, sulking. "Ok," he said.

"He is coming back. Soon, most likely. He wouldn't have left my collar on, or given you one, too, if he wasn't."

"I know. He's going to make me beat you again. I am so..."

"Just shut up, Roger." She wanted to be nice and vicious toward the man in equal measure. "My point is; we can't wait anymore. We have to chance it."

"We'll die. He'll kill us."

"We might, but do you really think we are getting out of here alive anyway? You saw what he did to that woman. I was hoping that there would be a chance to escape — that he would screw up – but we can't wait anymore. He is escalating."

"Yeah. I guess."

"So, *we* have to have a plan."

"I guess," he solemnly said.

"When he comes for us, he will bind our hands like last time. The second, the very fucking moment, that we are both free and close enough, we jump him. I'll grab his left arm, you grab his right. I don't think he can kill us if he doesn't have hands. Get him to the ground and beat him worse than you ever beat me. Understand?"

"How will I know when? What if he gets loose?"

"Don't *let* him get loose. That isn't an option, understand? As far as when... Shit. If we go at the wrong time..."

"We could have a code word," Roger offered.

"There you go! A code word. One of us shouts it and we both pounce. What's the word?"

"You don't have one?"

"Well, you came up with the idea, Roger, you pick the word," she said.

"How about – *manatee*?"

"What the hell is wrong with you? How is that a code word? You want me to shout *manatee* at the top of my lungs so I can get weirdly embarrassed before I probably die?"

"It was my wife's favorite animal. She had pictures and stuffed manatees all over the place," he said, beginning to tear up again.

"Okay, okay! *Manatee* it is. Just stop with the crying. So, the millisecond that one of us sees the opportunity, shout out the code word, and we go for it. Deal?"

"Yeah, deal."

Lucy finally had hope. It was tiny, just a speck of light meandering through the shadows, but it was there. She doubted that she could really count on Roger for anything, but he was her only option. Like it or not, he was her partner in this and she would do her best to believe in him.

Worthless as he was.

Hope has a tendency to wane when time is in play. It was eons before Edward returned. Roger took a long nap, but Lucy refused to allow herself to let her guard down until her vision began to blur. A few times, she had thought she saw movement to the side, but when she turned it was gone. The ghosts that haunted her must not be having as easy a time coming out now that she had gotten more food and water. Still, the thrill of excitement was gone, replaced by the disappointment that is a plan sitting on a shelf for too long.

Even so, when the door clicked, Lucy was quick to whisper, "Ready?"

She didn't get a response, but held onto the remaining hope with a vice grip.

Edward gave the two of them some water, then began to unfasten Lucy from the table.

This is it. Get ready. Fucking manatee. Whatever. Scream it the moment you see a window.

It wasn't until she was free and standing on her own that she noticed Edward's demeanor. He wasn't the mother crazed version she was expecting. He was regular Edward One. He let her stand there as he lit a cigarette and leaned against the curtain.

"You've got the collar on, so I guess you won't give me any trouble," he said. "Those things are brutal."

"So, I've been told," she responded.

"This is taking longer than I expected."

"Oh? Maybe I should try to speed it along. Give me a knife, I'll just slit my throat and you can leave me here."

"Jesus, calm down. You are a tense one."

Lucy laughed. "Yeah, I'm a bit on edge."

"Alright, come on," Edward said. "Follow me."

Roger stood, his chains rattling with desperation. "What about me?"

"What *about* you?"

Edward placed his palm on the small of her back, but the energy from his fingers wasn't the same as it had been before. There was no malice, no sex in his touch.

He led her to the door, then closed it behind them. She was in the hallway, this time fully lit. The walls were light green and trimmed in distressed wood. Lucy couldn't tell if the wood was old, or simply fabricated to appear that way. They skipped the room with the second table and went straight to the dining room. There were no faux candles or flowers, just an empty room that had grown musty in the short time since she had spilled blood on the giant rug beneath the long table.

He didn't take her to the table, but turned to the left to a door that had been obscured by the dark last she was in the room. Edward pulled a keyring from his pocket, weighted with enough keys to operate a prison. It took him a moment to find the right one and he turned away from her as he searched. He was paying her no attention, and Lucy knew this was a chance; a moment in time to force the hand of fate.

She remained still.

He was so nonchalant about her, it made her feel that he knew something that she did not. Maybe the danger of the collar wasn't as simple as she had thought. Could she chance it?

The door was open, and his eyes back on her before she could make the choice.

Inside was a beautifully decorated parlor. A massive chandelier gave the room a sparkly glow, casting shadows like fingers probing the light. Along an entire wall was a massive, vintage bar; fully stocked. The remainder of the room was filled with chairs, small tables holding up intricate lamps, an elaborately old chaise lounge; it only lacked an older woman smoking a cigarette extended in a silver holder and spewing drivel about what life was like when she was young and beautiful.

Edward walked ahead, near the bar, and as he passed the last stool, spun it to face her.

"Have a seat."

Lucy didn't know what was happening. Why was this room here? It was odd enough that there was a massive dining room inside an office building, but now the bizarre dream had spread into new rooms.

"What would you like?"

"What?" she asked.

"What's your drink?"

Lucy walked over to the waiting barstool and raised her body into the seat. Spinning back toward the bar, with Edward across from her, she said, "Long Island?"

"You don't seem sure. You can have whatever you want. It isn't poison or anything."

"Long Island is fine."

Edward grabbed several bottles from the top shelf and went to work. He was meticulous, getting the mixture perfect. When he placed the drink on the bar in front of her, it was perfectly mixed with a divine brown to yellow gradient. It took her a moment to reach for the drink, still fearing a hidden danger, but when she finally tasted her first sip, it was heavenly. Not just because she hadn't had anything but water for days, but because the mixture was spot on. Edward had gone light on the sweet and sour, just as she preferred.

"This is good," she stated, after a large swallow.

"I'm glad. I know things are hard for you."

God, what is your fucking game?

"Yeah, it's hell. How about you let me go?"

"I can't do that. You are here for a reason."

"Why?"

"I don't know. Stop asking me about it, or I'll take you back now."

Edward poured himself a neat glass of a bourbon she had never heard of. Lucy imagined it was a bottle only sold to the super rich, probably made with the fermented tears of unicorns and diamond dust. He downed it in two successive swallows, undoubtedly too used to the taste to savor it.

Lucy downed half her drink in the time that Edward poured two more for himself. She was becoming tipsier than she anticipated, probably due to her weakness and lack of food. She wasn't hungry at the moment, but her body wouldn't catch back up for a long time.

"What is this place?" she asked, her vision beginning to slow.

"Home."

"You live here?"

"No."

Not understanding, Lucy thought to inquire further, but Edward walked around her and sat in one of the parlor chairs. He lit a cigarette and smoked without regard for her. Lucy spun around in her stool to face him, leaving the remainder of her drink on the bar. It was good, but she couldn't risk it. As she spun a presence at the end of the bar caught her eye. Todd was there, hunched over, head on the bar. An empty glass was still in his hand and he wasn't moving.

Part of her wanted to ask Edward if he could see the man, thinking that maybe he was insane enough to see into her own hallucinations. That was a silly thought.

Just ignore him. He can't hurt you.

"So, what can we talk about?" she asked Edward, leaving Todd in her peripheral.

"I don't know. I have to be careful."

"Are you afraid of him?"

"Who?" Edward asked.

"The man inside you," she said.

He snickered and took another drag, then put the smoke out in a brass ashtray. He sat forward in his chair, and put his elbows to his knees; hands gripping his head for a moment before smoothing his hair.

"What kind of question is that?"

"Do you know what he will do, or is it always a surprise?"

"Stop."

"Who is in charge, him or you?"

"Shut up!"

She had him rattled and now had to decide if she should push further or back off. Speaking with him felt like flipping a knife into the air, catching it again and again, praying to find the handle each time.

"I've seen what he's capable of. You can stop it."

Edward didn't have anything further to say as he lit another cigarette. She watched him pull the nicotine into his lungs, ash growing longer, covering the orange firefly at the tip. He extinguished the cigarette halfway down, walked over to Lucy, and took the stool next to her. Her heart skidded on her sternum as he leaned in close, their eyes connected.

"I hope it turns out ok for you, I really do, but right now you need to know a few things. First, you are being watched, so don't try anything. Second, I have this for you," he said, pulling a card from his back pocket and setting it on the bar, before standing again and walking to a door on the far side of the parlor.

"Anything else?" Lucy asked.

"You're wrong," Edward said, lighting another smoke. "You have absolutely no idea what he is capable of."

The door slammed behind him.

Lucy looked at the card. Scrawled in a messy hand.

One word: *Mother*.

Fuck you, Edward. Just, fuck you.

She took the card into her left hand and flipped it over, then placed it back down. She raised her drink, and drained the second half. The liquor was smooth on her throat, warm in her belly. She looked over to Todd but he was gone, glass still sitting on the bar. The pain in her face and body was a tad bit better, but her mind was racing. The newest note sent her mind tumbling down a mountainside.

Feel free to explore.
Dinner is at 7pm.

All my love,
Edward.

Lucy was frozen. She was just shoved head first into freedom, she didn't know what to do with it. Was she to walk around the building until 7pm? Just as she realized that she had no way to know the time, she saw the antique clock against the far wall.

It was 6:20. She had no way of knowing if that was in the morning or night, but she doubted that she would be taken off her leash for an entire twelve hours.

Just get up and go. Worst case, you get electrocuted and die horribly.

Lucy's mind was swampy with alcohol. The drink was hitting her hard, and she felt like the first time she had managed to get a drink as a child. She was fourteen, two of her friends convinced her to sneak out one night. One of the girls had a cousin that was going to get them some booze from the convenience store.

MD 20/20. Mad dog. The single worst drunk a person can feel. Just a few drinks of that liquid garbage felt similar to how she felt now. A few more drinks, and she was like old silly putty that had seen far better days. Her father had to pick her up from her friend's house, and she feared the worst.

He didn't punish her in the way a normal father would–at least as she understood the dealings of other fathers. There was no scolding, yelling, or physical punishment. She was not grounded. Instead, she was tasked with cleaning the garage. Not the following day, but the very night that she was caught. It was hell.

He had told her, "The lesson is, you can do whatever you want, but there is always the chance that it's going to make your life harder."

She took a few more plunges into the world of underage drinking, but never again let it go that far. To this day, Lucy had felt nothing like that again, but now she was finding it terribly difficult to move effectively.

Her weak body, teamed with a compromised mind, made each step a chess move— carefully calculated, and often sacrificial. She made the arduous journey to the door that Edward had left through. His final cigarette had not been extinguished properly, and the smoke was making her nauseous. She gagged, then gagged again. Sour liquid rose through her esophagus and settled on the back of her tongue, causing a flavor that could only be described as boiling, acidic shit.

When Lucy made it to the door, she took a rest and leaned her back against the wall. Drinking the remainder of her Long Island Iced Tea was a massive lapse in judgement, and she only hoped that the effects would wear down before dinner was served.

I wouldn't want to puke on Edward's precious plastic bird carcass.

She opened the door and practically collapsed, but not from inebriation. In fact, the sight before her served to sober her somewhat. It was a house. Not a few odd rooms built by a mother-fucking killer, but an entire house built within the walls of a skyscraper. It was beyond comprehension.

There was an elaborate, winding staircase straight ahead with a red runner, and an ornate wooden railing. The ceiling was at least 30 feet up and intricately carved in gold. A grand piano sat off to the left with a magenta carpet beneath. There was a marble bust of a man she did not recognize, and several other carved sculptures that were more abstract. The room itself was far larger than her own apartment.

Hell, Lucinda, this is four of your apartments.

There were several archways to other rooms on each side of this one, and Lucy found herself overwhelmed. Sitting down on the hard, marbled floor, she wrapped her arms around her mid-section. She wasn't going to vomit, but her insides felt cold, and she was beginning to shiver. On the outside, her skin began to bleed sweat and she imagined what it would look like to see her from the very top of the stairs. How small and pathetic she would appear.

"You are being watched," she had been told. Someone out there could see her spasming body drip salty sweat onto their perfect marble floor.

Get up Lucinda. Get up. Your time is ticking away, you have to learn what you can.

More and more, the logical voice in her mind wasn't her own, but her father's. Even now, so many years later, she still didn't want to let him down. She knew that it wasn't possible that he was looking down on her from above because he was too busy burning alive below, but still, she wanted to make him proud. As if on cue, her father appeared.

Across the slick floor, near one of the archways, he stood impatiently. Lucy could see the reflection of his body in the buffed marble, distorted like a light wind blowing through a clear stream.

Lucy rose to her feet, surprisingly without incident. She was still feeling the effects of the drink and the shock to her mind, but she was resolved. She would move forward, lest her father scold her.

After more steps than one person should ever have to walk across a single room, she stood under an arch with elaborate scroll work accenting the entrance to the next room. Her father sighed and motioned for her to enter through the arch.

She would call this new place a living room if it were in her own abode, but here, among the furnishings of the rich, she assumed there was a fancier word. Chairs, couches, and love seats were arranged in a square pattern, with a stone and glass table in the center. On the left side was a fireplace that she was convinced she could park a Fiat within, on the right was a wall covered in framed photographs.

Her father sat down in one of the chairs, leaning forward with his elbows on his knees, fingers touching.

"I don't understand you," he said. "You had more than one chance back there."

"I couldn't. The collar is elec…"

"I know all about the collar! It's no excuse. You are going to die if you don't do something to stop it. How long do you think you can survive on protein bars and occasional drops of water? How many more punches to the face do you think you can endure?"

He isn't real Lucinda. Ignore him.

"You can't ignore me," he said. "You know that."

"Dad, just leave me alone. Please."

Her eyes wanted to close but she knew that would be rude. She was to listen until he was through.

"Maybe sometimes there just isn't a way out."

"Spoken like a true loser, letting a bad situation defeat you." He stood. "Have it your way girl, but I'll be back. You need me."

He walked away until he suddenly wasn't there, leaving her alone and shivering.

Lucy noticed a picture on the wall. There were many, but this one caught her eye. A young Edward, dressed in a blue graduation gown and holding a rolled paper tied with string. Lucy walked to the picture and almost smiled. Edward hadn't changed at all since high school, save a more prominent jaw line, and elaborately toned physique. He appeared an innocent young man, destined for greatness on a path lined with cash.

She looked around at the other photos, some with Edward, but a lot of others without. When she saw the picture of the woman, there was no mistaking his mother. Edward more than resembled her. She had a beauty that would make anyone blush, but within her eyes, Lucy couldn't help but see pain. Perhaps she was projecting herself onto the photo, but behind the smile filled with perfectly lined teeth, Lucy thought the woman seemed timid. Afraid. Her eyes were the same shade of empty as Edward's were during his lapses.

She didn't know why it had taken her so long to realize what she was seeing. The oddness of it all must have wiped her common sense. This was *his* house. Not a room or two, but the entire thing, meticulously recreated, or instead moved, piece by piece, into this hidden space. How much room would it take to create this within the building, and how could Edward have possibly made it happen without anyone knowing?

Do they not know? Someone must, unless he killed them all. Oh, fuck. Get it together Lucinda! It doesn't matter how the house got here; it only matters why. You are being held captive by a man that is so attached to his childhood, he built this.

She sat down on one of the loveseats. It wasn't remotely comfortable, but expensive furniture often isn't. After a few moments of staring at the wall of photographs, she leaned over to her left and lay with her knees tucked up against her torso. She had about a half hour before she was expected for dinner, and exploring the house didn't seem so important anymore. It would be like wandering through the mind of a psychopath, twisting and turning through the synapses of his youth and discovering nothing but questions.

It was best that she rest, sober up, and prepare.

He would have her alone.

He would have her at a disadvantage.

He would have to die.

Lucy sat for so long at the dining room table that she was beginning to think that maybe she had gotten the location wrong. What if Edward had expected dinner in a different place? Her mind was inventing scenarios in which a simple fuck-up would get her killed. She had made sure to get to the dining room earlier than seven, just to be sure, but it had to be time by now.

It had to be.

There was no clock that she could see from her chair at the table, but that may have been because it was so dark. Other than just a couple of wall sconces giving off a low glow, there was no light. The candle lights that had previously illuminated the room with their fake flickering were not lit.

Then, all at once, they turned on, and the room was awash with wispy beams. Lucy closed her eyes to shield them from the sudden change, and when she opened them again, she found Edward standing on the far side of the room. That portion of the dining room was still quite dark, but she could make him out in the shadows, and now wondered if he had always been there. Watching her. Her core was cold with nervousness, her mind warm with murderous intent, but she let neither show.

"Hey. Let's eat. I'm starved," she said. He didn't move toward her, so she continued, "Edward, can you hear me?"

She didn't think that he could. He was in his transition. The Edward that she had shared a drink with must have come here, awaiting the change within him. She wondered if that Edward was aware of how often he changed, and if so, did he feel like a prisoner in his own shell? Had he kidnapped himself just as he had her?

Lucy was rapping her fingers on the table top when Edward finally walked over. She sat up straight in her chair, bracing herself for what might come. The light from the electric candles flickered against his face as he approached, reminding Lucy of the hell she was in. Edward was no Devil, but they could have easily been roommates in college.

He circled the table and stood to her left. Lucy dared not look at him, keeping her sight on the wall where Edward once stood. He didn't speak a word, but instead, grabbed her chair and spun it around to face him. She still made an effort to avoid eye contact, but when he dropped to his knees, she was locked in their gaze again.

Hit him.

"I tried to talk to Father, but he wouldn't listen. I'm so sorry, Mother. I thought I could talk sense into him, and he would stop hurting us."

Kick him in the balls.

"We can't live with his pain anymore," Edward continued. "There is only one choice left to us."

Kick him in the balls, then pin him down at the wrists.

Edward laid his head in her lap and was beginning to sniffle and sob. He reached up to hold her, resting his hands on her lower back, then moving them further down.

Beat him in the head with something. Knock him out. Tie him up.

His eyes burned when they looked back into hers. It was so hard to reconcile the look this man was giving her, with the killer she knew him to be. She envisioned the whip wrapping around that woman's throat, and the sharp sound it made when he yanked it back. This man on his knees, he is the person that did that, yet his eyes held no hate. No evil. He was a simple man looking for absolution and guidance from his mother.

Rip out his eyes.

Edward stood and placed a hand out for her. With slight hesitation, she took it and stood. Their bodies were but a half inch apart, she could feel the heat radiating from him and she wondered if he could feel the ice in her blood. Saying nothing, he walked her through the swinging door.

Expecting to find a kitchen, Lucy instead found virtually nothing. It was a room with an island in the center and a few kitchen-esque items, but certainly not a place to cook a meal. In one corner, she saw a trash can filled with the plastic food that was served to her last time, as well as all the platters. She scanned the room: trash, salt shaker, and what looked to be a knife near the sink on the other side.

Grab the knife. Stab him.

The island was blocking her path to the sink, and Edward was still holding one of her hands. She wouldn't be able to get to the knife and use it before he could kill her.

They didn't linger in this room, as Edward led her right to another door. On the other side, was the same giant entryway that she had seen earlier. The marble floor felt cold on her feet, and she wished to God that he would let go of her hand.

A large vase was standing just outside the door, filled with long, knotted sticks and fake foliage. It wasn't to her taste, but fit well within the confines of the entryway.

Hit him in the face with the vase.

Edward continued to lead her, now to the base of the stairs. Closer up, Lucy could see that the red runner was actually rather shabby, as if a million feet had stomped the life out of it. Edward led her up the stairs.

She used her free hand to hold onto the rail, as her body was still feeling quite weak, her head was starting to blur again. Noticing that she was having trouble, Edward slowed down and let her catch her breath. He smiled at her and then continued on.

At the top of the stairs was one long, massive hallway that extended in both directions. The walls were lined with huge paintings, mostly portraits, in elaborately decorated golden frames. The picture at the very middle was of a man that had a definite resemblance to Edward, and as she looked into the painted man's eyes, Edward took notice.

"You were always so fond of Grandfather," he said.

"What? I mean, yeah, I suppose I was."

Edward proceeded down the right hallway. The walk was a long one, and Lucy's thoughts were overwhelming.

Push him into that small table.

Slam his face into one of these paintings.

Hell, just pull your hand away and run. Die running.

It was at the second to last door on the left side of the hallway that Edward stopped. He let her go and began to rifle through his massive keyring.

Run!

He pushed the door open and motioned for her to enter first. Inside was a bedroom furnished for royalty. Not a single piece of furniture could have possibly been made this century, or last. The four-poster bed stood as a giant, enormous yet graceful in the center of the room. Lucy had never seen a bed so large or ornate. A massive wardrobe adorned the right wall, and a vanity the left. The glass on the vanity's mirror was tarnished, but the wood was exquisite.

Candlestick, sheets, hairbrush, shoes. She couldn't find anything to help her.

Lucinda, in the bedroom, with the candlestick.

Edward led her to the bed and bid her to sit.

"It is okay, Mother. No one will hurt you tonight. Father is away, and I will take care of you."

I hate you.

"Just lie back," he said, gently pushing her over. Her head sank into the down pillows, and she was ashamed at how good it felt. Whatever came next, she would not forget the moment that her neck softened into feathery luxury.

Click.

He had her left arm held up, and locked one side of a pair of handcuffs around her wrist.

"No. Wait a minute. What are you doing?"

"No need to fret, Mother. I told you that I would take care of you, and I will."

Edward fastened the other end of the handcuffs to the bed-post and stood tall, satisfied. He walked quickly out of sight, and Lucy immediately began to pull at the cuffs. They were secure, but at least she still had one arm free. She could still fight him off. She *could*.

When Edward returned, he walked all the way around the bed, then climbed in and walked on his hands and knees over to her. Lucy could see the needle in his clenched hand, and somehow took comfort in knowing that she would soon be marooned in sweet oblivion. She wouldn't have to face whatever happened.

You can still fight.

He nestled into her in a similar fashion as last time. Her body shivered, and she was clenching her toes. Edward laid his head in the nook of her armpit and pulled her hand around to rest on his chest. She closed her eyes then, preparing to flee to the protection of her forest.

"I love you so much, Mom. I only want you to be happy," he said to her, as she drifted away. Part of her wanted to come back to the moment and tell him off. To tell him that his mother hates him, that he disgusts her. She felt the needle poke into her skin, and it was a welcome sting. She wouldn't need her forest, and she wouldn't need to confront the man. She would sleep.

Pure, unabated sleep.

"I will kill him for us," Edward said, just as she drifted away.

CHAPTER 11

Two days in, she didn't think she would make it. Despite all of her father's teachings, Lucy had a hell of a time navigating through the dense trees. She couldn't be sure how straight a path she had cut, but she felt like she was veering west, no matter how hard she tried to turn eastward. If she veered further west, then she would never make it to the edge of the forest. There was nothing over there except more trees for miles.

And bears.

Let's not think about those.

If she took a perfectly northern path she would eventually hit the river, then she could just follow that east to where her father would be waiting, but the river takes a sharp turn north about a mile away from where she was headed. If she veered too far west, she would never meet the river, or at least not for a couple more days.

"You've got the sun, and you've got your wits. Stop second guessing every little thing. The trees will guide you if you just know what they're saying."

Her father's words were beginning to ring empty, and she couldn't stop second and triple guessing herself. All of the navigational tricks she had been taught were now seemingly inaccessible in her mind. She had no fear of dying out here, as her father could certainly track her down in a breath, but she was letting her old man down, and that was worse than death.

That afternoon, she stumbled through the trees into a clearing. A large pond sat idle, and the sun was shining bright on her left. She really *was* going the right way.

Lucy sat down on a fallen tree not far from the pond to take a rest. Every now and then, a gentle southeasterly breeze would ripple the water, making the dragonflies take flight to avoid the waves. As a branch cracked in the distance, Lucy looked up as two deer poked their bodies timidly into the clearing. They were both young does, and Lucy's jaw quivered at their beauty. She watched them slowly move forward to drink. One would take her fill, while the other kept watch.

Lucy would return to that pond many more times before graduating and moving on with her life, but she never again saw anything as breathtaking. When the deer left, she picked herself back up, and headed in the direction that was positively northeast.

She was exposed. She hadn't yet opened her eyes for fear that the light would hurt her head, on top of what the drug had already accomplished, but she could still *feel*. The dress was gone, replaced by some kind of long sleeve garment. A sweater most likely. The cold air against her thighs tingled the knowledge that she wore nothing below.

Had he raped her? She didn't feel as though he had, but then she didn't exactly know what it would feel like. She definitely didn't feel as if she had sex, and there was no soreness as she would imagine. Still, there was no way to be sure. Edward never did things as another might.

Let it go, Lucinda. He either did, or didn't. There is nothing you can do about it now. Focus.

She was becoming much quicker at dismissing atrocity and that didn't sit well. It was true that there was nothing she could do after the fact, but shouldn't she care more?

No. Not now. You can sort out everything when this is over.

A gurgling pop emanated from her left. Roger sat hunched over, arms splayed across the floor, blood thickly covering much of his head. She would think him dead if it wasn't for the sounds of gargled blood, the slight lifting of his body with each slow breath.

Even with Roger in his current state, Lucy couldn't help but feel embarrassed by her lack of clothing. She looked down, just to verify that she hadn't gone crazy. She hadn't. There was nothing but a tuft of hair and magnificently pale, unshaven legs. There were no bruises that she could see.

"What happened to you, Roger?" she asked, trying to sound sympathetic.

He twitched a bit, and his breathing seemed to get a little more rapid. The sounds spilling from his mouth grew slowly into discernable words, and he lifted his head. The gore covered him in globs. It was like a special effects artist had spilled their whole kit on top of him.

"My god, Roger. Are you going to make it?"

"I...fu...fucking hope not," he said, as a long, thin stream of blood dropped from the side of his mouth, mixing with the pool that had already accrued on his lap. Each breath made a new sound, each small movement a cringe.

"When did he do that?"

"Not that long. Hour. Two. After he brought y...you back."

Lucy waited a while before making Roger speak again. She knew that each word was painful for him. She felt less modest knowing that he couldn't possibly focus in on her nudity. She felt a twinge of guilt for thinking of herself when he was so destroyed, but then she thought of his fists flying at her; felt his knuckles gouge at her skin. Roger would have to cope.

"Did he say anything when he beat you?"

"Yeah."

Lucy waited a moment, impatiently.

"Well? What did he say?"

"He said that I would never be allowed to hurt you again."

Roger hadn't moved in some time, so Lucy assumed he was asleep. His death rattles were finally starting to subside, and he had wiped some of the blood off with his shirt. They spent hours in silence and Lucy thought she had caught Roger peering at her a couple of times, though she chose to let it slide. She figured she may be wrong, and if not, he probably could use a thrill – if what she had on display could still be considered thrilling after all this.

She thought back to a time in her marriage when she wasn't convinced of its doom; to a day spent outside among the trees. Not the forest of her father, but a small wood on the edge of a park by their home. At that point, she still considered it a home, not the slice of Hell that it truly was.

Todd had been sweet that whole day, and in the privacy of the trees, he leaned her against a particularly thick trunk, lowering her pants. Todd dropped to his knees and serviced her in a way that he had never before. When she had climaxed, he stood and told her, "You have the best pussy I have ever seen."

"Ugh, don't say that. You know I hate that word."

He laughed and apologized. That had been a great day. When she still thought he hung the moon, and he still thought she was a person deserving of love and respect. Just a few years later, he wouldn't find her pussy so wonderful needing to hurt it to derive any pleasure.

Lucy tried to close her eyes and sleep – to try and dream of nicer things, but she was interrupted by the sound of the door.

Edward had returned with a small pile of clothes in his hand.

"I am so sorry you had to wait, Mom. You *urinated* in your clothes again, so I took care of it for you." He whispered the word, as if an audience might hear of her incontinence.

He began to unclasp the restraints around her ankles. Lucy imagined herself kicking the man squarely in the nose, but she remembered the collar. It was still around her neck, though as time passed she wondered if she would get to a point that death would be worth it, just to hurt him once.

He knelt down and held out the same pair of panties that he had made her wear under the blue dress. Gently placing her feet into the leg holes, he smiled up at her. He continued to lock eyes as he slowly raised the underwear up her legs, finally replacing her modesty – as well as mesh ever could.

He lingered there, his face an inch from her crotch. When he pushed his nose into her, she cut the scream off before it could manifest. He inhaled her deeply, just as the other Edward would inhale his cancer smoke, then grabbed her jeans.

He pulled them up without further invasion of her, replaced the restraints, then stood.

"I took care of it, Mother. I finally did!" he said, excited as a puppy. "He won't do it again. He won't hurt you."

Edward waited for an answer, his expression frozen.

"Thank you," Lucy said.

"You never have to thank me. Never. I love you."

He kissed her cheek, this time as a son would, then stepped back. Edward switched the light to orange, and opened the red curtain. The moment that the curtain was drawn, Bonnie's voice erupted over the intercom.

"Mr. Wolcroft, I am so sorry. I tried and tried, but Agent Henderson is here." She said, then there was a shuffling sound. "Stop, you can't just barge..."

Agent Henderson burst into the room, looking around.

"Where is he?" he demanded.

"See, I told you he probably wasn't in. Now leave. I'll tell him you stopped by."

"I don't think so. I think I'll stay put and wait," the agent said, as he plopped down into a seat while simultaneously grabbing an old issue of GQ from a side table. Bonnie looked completely baffled, but said nothing. She slammed the door behind her, the only way she could adequately voice her dissatisfaction with the man's behavior.

"He's back," Lucy said, unable to contain her glee.

"Yes, he is. Don't worry, Mom, I'll get rid of him and then we can spend some time together."

"No rush," she said, though she didn't think he was listening. He was out the door and back in his office within a couple of minutes this time.

"Sorry to keep you waiting," Edward said, as he walked by Henderson and sat at his desk. "I can't talk long I'm afraid. So many meetings today."

"Oh, that's just fine, Edward. Can I call you 'Edward'? I figure I'm in here so often, we should be on a first name basis by now."

"Call me whatever you like, Agent Henderson. Now why are you here?"

"Right. I just wanted to let you know that I found your car and I'm keeping it safe for you. Well, we did rip it up a little, but it couldn't be helped."

"Is that all?" Edward asked, impatiently.

"Mostly, but I also wanted to let you know that I'll have another piece of paper for you soon. I'd like to have a look around this place, probably your home, too. I realize that may be a little upsetting to hear, so there will be plenty of guys downstairs to keep an eye on you. Make sure you don't run away or anything."

"There is nothing I am hiding. I don't know why you persist," Edward said, his voice deliberate, hands clenching tightly.

"I sure do hope that is true. You, sir, are a pillar of the world, I'd hate to see you fall."

"You can leave now."

"I suppose so. I'll let you get to your meeting. I can't imagine what your job is like, running this corporation like you do. Boggles my mind," Henderson said, standing. He made the hat tipping gesture, then walked away, stopping in front of the shark tank. "These are magnificent creatures you have here. It's a shame they aren't in the wild. What do you feed them?"

"Meat."

"Yeah, I guess that's what you would need to feed something like that. All right then, good day to you."

Without further discussion, Henderson left, and Edward slumped into his chair. Lucy watched as he stared into space, waiting for that moment that he would stand and leave the office, longing for those few minutes of freedom that it would take him to come and take her again.

"Don't worry, there is nothing he can do to us," Edward said as he unfastened the final strap. "Please come with me, Mother."

"Where are we going?" Lucy asked.

"Home. Dad won't be there tonight. He is still on his trip. I can't wait until his associates see the black eye I gave him," he said, laughing.

"What are we going to do at home?"

Edward didn't notice her question, instead holding his hand out for her to lead the way. She led them out to the hallway, through the dining room, into the parlor, then out to the large foyer. The lights in that part of the house were blinding compared to the orange of her own world.

"Up the stairs," Edward said.

Turning toward him, Lucy said, "Why don't we do something else tonight? How about we watch TV or play a game?"

"You've never liked TV! Don't be silly. Come on."

Lucy spun back around, sighed, then walked to the staircase. Her mind was slashing through one idea after another, unable to settle on any that had a chance of improving her situation. She took the steps slowly, desperately hoping that an idea would come to her if she postponed for long enough. Edward was patient with her, smiling anytime she looked to him.

"I'm not feeling very well," she said.

"After you lie down, I will get some medicine."

They walked to the same room as before and inside felt cold and humid. Lucy's skin became clammy and sweat beaded her brow. He had to prod her several times before she took the last few steps to the bed, but when she got there she laid with her arm above her head, resting near the bedpost. She didn't have an idea, so she would submit this time, already thinking of the hawks flying above the trees.

She could feel the sheets beneath her dampen from her sweat as Edward cuffed her hand to the bed. He reached up and laid the outer edges of his fingers on her bruised face, tears beginning to form in his eyes.

"I am so sorry that he hurt you like that. I promise he never will again."

"I'm sure," Lucy said.

"Really! I mean it this time, mom. If he ever lays a hand on you again, I will kill him. I swear."

"Your promises don't mean shit, *son*. Not a damned thing. Now do what you are going to do, so I can get some sleep."

Her words came out more forceful than she would have thought possible. On the inside, she was a mess of fear, anger, and sadness. Her mind couldn't even begin to settle on the proper emotion for any given moment. If he didn't rape her the last time, he was going to now. She was sure of it. There was nothing she could do. She should have taken any moment before this and tried to get away. Death sounded like a pleasant experience as Edward looked at her with crying eyes.

His smile drooped and faded, and his pupils abruptly doubled in size. Edward began to pace frantically, waving his arms around in the air in no discernable pattern. Not knowing what to expect next, Lucy raised her legs up to her body as tight as she could in a futile attempt at safety. Edward was rushing around the room, his arms knocking a vase from the nightstand; his face turning apple red.

Then, he abruptly stopped and sat down in a chair by the vanity. He reached in his pocket for a pack of cigarettes and lit one. Lucy relaxed a little as she realized the other Edward was with her now.

He said, "You are in a tight spot."

"You think?"

"What are you going to do?"

I'm going to kill you when I get the chance.

"No idea."

"Well, I suggest you come up with something, because I don't know how long you have."

He meant he didn't know how long *he* would be there. Lucy was having such a hard time keeping it straight. She kept telling herself to wait for her moment and strike, but each moment seemed like a strange new carnival ride. How could she see an opportunity if she couldn't understand the moment? How many had she already missed?

No. It doesn't matter. You will know what to do when it's time. Have faith.

Lucy didn't think that any internal pep talk would work this time. There was no way out.

"I probably shouldn't even bother to ask you to unlock the cuffs, huh?"

"It would be a waste of precious time," Edward said, taking a drag.

"Then talk. Say something to me. Explain something that I don't know, which is almost everything. Why is this happening? Do you just have a fucked-up love for your mom? Is that really all this is?"

"Don't talk about my mother," he said. "She was a damned whore that tore my father apart. She pushed and pushed, and it drove him crazy. Drove *me* crazy. You know about it— it was in the papers."

"No, I don't know."

"Well, it doesn't matter. My mother isn't going to help you, and neither is my dad. Hell, he would probably slap you just for being in his house."

"Why?"

"Why? It's obvious. Because you're trash. He would never associate with the likes of you, and certainly would never let one of you touch his sheets."

"Fuck you! I'm not trash."

"Hey, don't get me wrong. I feel for you, I really do. But, I have a different outlook than he did. He saw no reason to lower himself, whereas, I know that sometimes it's a necessary evil."

Lucy couldn't believe the words, yet they made perfect sense. Edward was some big, rich CEO or something. Of course, he would look down on her, she just never imagined that there really were people that looked *that* far down.

"Why have I never heard of Edward Wolcroft?"

"Because I like it that way. You see, there are two kinds of rich. There are those that run companies and are in all the magazines. Then there are those that own the companies that run all the others. The companies you would have never heard of. Unless you read up on business, you wouldn't have any idea. We don't hog the media like some people do. There is far more power in anonymity than there will ever be in money alone.

You won't find us on any lists of rich names. We are the unspoken top of the food chain."

"You have a very high opinion…"

"Not opinion! Don't misunderstand me. This is simply truth. There are those that run for President, and those that run *the* President. Those that make a billion dollars a year, and those that spend a billion just for kicks. We are the power behind the power."

"So, I should just give up?"

"I wouldn't suggest it. You seem stronger than most people I've seen. You may find a way out, but I promise – the game is just beginning."

"You would think this was just a game, wouldn't you?" she asked.

"Of course, it is, but I don't know how long it will last. Feds are on to me. I can't imagine I will talk my way out of this one." He took a long drag, and put the cigarette out on the vanity. "Time's up. Maybe I'll see you again, but I would be surprised."

"Wait, where are you going?"

But, he didn't go anywhere. He simply stopped being— eyes glassy, shoulders slouched. Lucy struggled with the handcuffs, making her hand as slim as she could, tugging hard. The pain was immense, but she felt like there was some give. The notion spurred her on.

This pain is nothing.

Edward interrupted her struggle quicker than she had anticipated. The transformation usually took five or ten minutes, but it couldn't have been more than two this time. She jumped as she caught a glimpse of him walking back to her side of the bed. She hadn't even heard him move.

"Did you hear that?" Edward asked.

"Um, no."

He was oblivious to her attempts at escape.

"I heard someone drive up. Were you expecting someone?"

"Not a soul, psycho."

"I wonder if Dad came home early. He wasn't supposed to get in until tomorrow. Shit, I hope it isn't him."

"Why don't you go and see, son of mine," Lucy suggested.

"I will. I will protect you. I swear it."

Edward leaned over and kissed her lips tenderly, then rushed out of the room, slamming the door behind him. She didn't know what would happen next, but for now it was just her, a pair of handcuffs, and willpower.

Things were looking up.

CHAPTER 12

The pain in Lucy's hand reached a point that she couldn't over-come. Blood spilled down her arm and dripped over the bed. She wondered how Edward's father would feel about so much trash blood staining his expensive sheets. She knew that she had made progress in getting her hand out of the cuffs, but she had to take a break.

Tears lined her cheeks, mostly involuntary from the strug-gle. Edward had been gone a long time, and she was starting to wonder if he would come back today. Maybe she would get to have a semi-comfortable snooze in a real bed.

It's the little things.

She was able to keep time by a small clock on the far wall, and after a twenty-minute rest, she decided that, excruciating pain aside, she had to try harder. Edward had now been gone nearly two hours.

After just a couple minutes of squeezing and pulling, Lucy heard noises from outside the door. Roger was yelling. She could tell it was his voice, but couldn't make out the words until he got closer to the door.

"You leave her alone, you pig!"

The door burst open, and Roger tripped inside, pushed by the heel of Edward's shoe. His arms were tied behind his back and attached to a long chain. Edward held the other end. Roger was completely nude except for his collar, and his body still had an unhealthy amount of blood caked to it.

Edward had Roger stand at the foot of the bed and the man was crying. After unhooking the chain from his wrists, and undoing the restraint, Edward took a step back. Roger stood, a frumpy mess of aged skin and body hair, shivering and embarrassed.

"Father is home early. Isn't that wonderful, Mother?"

"Sure," she said.

"Go show your love for her, Father. Give her a kiss."

Roger didn't move so Edward took the end of the chain and lashed it across his belly. There was an instant reddening and Roger screeched.

"Go ahead," Edward insisted.

The naked man walked to the side of the bed, putting one hand over his penis, and leaned over to kiss Lucy on the forehead.

"You can do better, Father. I've seen you."

Roger leaned over a second time and pressed his lips to hers. His salty tears dripped down on her, and Lucy clenched her fists.

Don't throw up. Don't throw up.

"That's nice. Isn't that nice?" asked Edward. "Now, take her clothes off."

"What? No!" Lucy yelled, but Edward paid no attention.

Roger looked at Edward, then back at her. With the look of a defeated man, he reached for the button of her jeans. Still crying, he lowered the zipper and began to tug the jeans down her legs.

"Edward, you have to stop this now!" she shouted.

Edward stayed silent as Roger got her jeans to her feet, pulled them off, and then threw them to the floor. When he reached up and put his fingers under the elastic waist of her underwear, she tried to move her body away. His touch felt like cold Vaseline, and her mind flooded with thoughts of what might come.

"Edward, listen to me. I am your mother! You can't let this happen. You said so yourself."

Unable to move out of the reach of Roger's long arms, she relented. He pulled the skimpy panties down, then threw them near her pants. He stood and stared at her. She thought that he might have snapped, but then she saw his penis begin to rise.

"I'm so sorry," he told her.

She knew she shouldn't hate him for what he was doing, but she did anyway. She hated the man with every fiber, every vein pulsing pure fury through her system. He may apologize a thousand times, but his face and cock both told her otherwise. Maybe part of him was sorry, the rest considered himself lucky.

Edward said, "Keep going."

"I can't get the sweater off because of the handcuffs."

"Then just rip it! You are one of the most powerful men in the world. Take what you want."

He pulled up on the front of her sweater and began to try and rip the fabric. At first, it seemed like he was making no progress, but then the grating sound of tearing fibers. Roger managed to tear a hole across the entire front of the sweater, but the reinforced bottom proved more difficult.

"For fuck's sake," Edward said, then grabbed a pair of scissors from the vanity and handed them to Roger, "Finish."

He took the scissors and easily cut through the rest of the sweater. He cut down the length of the left arm so as to remove the full garment. Roger then used the scissors to snip the front of her bra, causing the elastic to snap away and reveal her breasts. He cut the shoulder straps, then pulled the pieces out from under her. She was completely exposed, and Roger stood completely erect.

"Now take her, Father. Take her the way I always hear you through the walls. It doesn't matter if she says no, does it? It never mattered to you."

"I don't want to do this," said Roger.

"Oh, yes you do! Just look at yourself," Edward shouted, motioning to Roger's crotch. "Now get on the bed and fuck your wife. Make her scream the way you like to do. Do the things that make me hate you."

Without further protest, Roger got on the bed at Lucy's feet. He took hold of both her ankles, and ran his hands up her legs, settling on the back of her thighs. As he positioned himself for what was to come, Lucy couldn't think straight. She couldn't let this happen. To think that she had been so nonchalant about this just a short while ago. She couldn't allow this man to rape her, damn the consequences.

Make a choice, Lucinda. Fight. Die fighting!

When she felt Roger push into her, everything suddenly became clear. Lucy lashed out with her free hand, punching Roger over and over in the chest. She swung her feet at him, making contact a couple of times, but Roger just spread her legs further apart. He reached up and pinned her arm to the bed, continuing to gyrate his hips with mechanical precision.

"Stop. Get the fuck off me! You can't do this!"

All Roger could say was, "I'm sorry."

"I'm sorry. I'm sorry. I'm sorry. I'm so…"

The chain landed on the top of Roger's head first, then flung forward and into his face, the final thick link crashing into his open mouth. Roger's eyes bugged, and he stopped his gyration. Blood began to free flow from his mouth down to her stomach, filling her belly button and running down her waist.

Edward swung the chain again, this time making contact with Roger's side, knocking the man over on the bed.

"I told you, you fucker. I told you! Never again."

Roger balled himself up as blow after blow of the chain crashed against his body, tenderizing him with agony. Crimson ribbons flew into the air with each swing, the sheets pooling below his twitching form.

When he stopped moving, Edward didn't stop swinging. Lucy looked away, unable to face the gore. She hated Roger, but she never wanted this.

When the swinging finally stopped, Lucy looked back to find that Roger's body was no longer on the bed, and Edward looked down to the floor at what Lucy could only imagine was a chewed-up pile of flesh. She cried, but she was out of tears to shed.

Edward dropped the chain and looked to her.

"I finally did it. I told you I would, and I did."

"You're sick."

"Aren't you proud of me, Mother? I freed you!"

"I..."

Any words that she might have come up with were blocked by shock. Lucy raised up as far as she could and pulled at the cuffs.

Edward looked genuinely hurt. He climbed up the foot of the bed and crawled over to the side of her. Lucy immediately began flailing again, her limbs flying in every direction, desperate to make contact. Her breathing was heavy, and her heart was pumping far too fast. She had to get away. She had to.

The man managed to grab hold of her legs with his own, pinning them to the bed. He then took her arm and held it down to her chest. His body curled around hers and he tried to lean in for a kiss. Lucy lashed open with chomping teeth, forcing a retreat.

"Fuck you! FUCK YOU! Let me go."

"This is our time. We can be together now. You and me. Just like I know you always wanted. I've wanted this forever, Mom. I love you so much."

He caressed her breasts, and she was just about to shout another round of obscenities in his direction, before she managed to stop and think.

You are his mother. His mother. Be his mother now.

"Edward, I love you, too." Her words were timid and shaky, but she got them out.

"I knew you did!"

"Of course, I do, Edward. I am your mother, and will always love you, but you are wrong. I do not want to *be* with you," she said, trying to remain calm in the face of her racing heart. "Not like that. I will never want to have sex with you. That is wrong and evil. Can't you see?"

"No, you love me. You want to be with me, I know you do. It was just Dad. He was in the way."

"No, Edward. Your father was a lot of things, but he wasn't in the way of you and I being together. I will never feel for you in that way."

He backed away from her, and despite the intense desire to hit and kick him, she stayed still. He backed away more quickly, and slipped in the pool of Roger's blood, his hand sliding to the end of the bed, face making a splash. When he raised his head again, it was slathered in dripping crimson and his eyes were pure panic. Crawling from the bed, he collapsed on the floor. When he stood again, he was a bloody mass of confusion.

"I killed him.," he said. "I killed him for you."

"I know. Thank you, that was sweet of you."

That set Edward off, and he began to slam his fist into the wall. He slammed himself into the furniture, screaming all the while, before finally becoming still. He looked once more at Lucy, and she smiled back at him.

He grabbed her pants from the floor, reached down and took hold of one of Roger's arms, and rushed out of the room, dragging the body along.

Lucy laid still as his screams grew more distant.

When she had finally made it to the rendezvous with her father, he was nowhere to be seen. Lucy had expected him to be waiting in his truck, doing a crossword puzzle, or reading a Tom Clancy novel, but there was nothing. There was also no sign that she could see that he had been there recently.

After waiting until the sun began to descend the sky, she decided that she would have to walk. What she hoped was the end of her journey; the end of her test, was now the beginning of another five-mile hike home.

She took the trip at a leisurely pace, proud of herself for what she had accomplished. She felt a glow and was truly content. The feeling made everything around her beautiful beyond belief. The air felt crisp and new against her skin, and the smells of the forest were so pure.

When she arrived back home, Lucy felt eighty pounds lighter. Then she heard the crying.

Her mother.

Lucy found her in the kitchen, face in her palms.

"What's wrong mom?" Lucy asked, putting her arm around the crying woman.

Her face was red, slathered in tears and snot.

"I saw him drive away."

"What are you talking about? Dad? Did something happen to Dad?"

"He left you a note. I opened it. Sorry."

On the table sat an envelope messily torn open, with a folded piece of paper, crumpled. It was damp when Lucy picked it up. She unfolded it carefully, scared of what she would find.

His words were brief, as they always had been.

I stayed until you were ready.
I can't anymore.

Lucy couldn't help but cry out as she finally got up the courage to push her thumb far enough. As the bone cracked, her blood lubricated hand slipped free. After sitting up, she tried her best to wipe the blood from her stomach, digging into her navel. Lucy had never felt so unclean. She looked at her left hand, thumb crunched over at an unnatural angle.

She took hold of the thumb and pulled, letting out another cry as it snapped back into place. The pain was a throbbing reminder that she was wasting time. She was free. Now was *her* time.

Even in his agitated state, Edward had managed to take her jeans away. He had no reason to leave her naked except for a sick power trip but it wasn't going to work. She didn't bother to put on the panties. Lucy had moved beyond modesty - the only thing left was survival. She put her ear to the door just to make sure she couldn't hear movement on the opposite side. Relatively sure that Edward was gone, she passed through the door and closed it quietly behind her. Now she had to find a way out.

Lucy knew that there were no other doors on this floor that could lead her out. After rushing the length of the hallway, she paused to carefully look around the corner before descending the stairs. When she got to the bottom, she realized that in a normal house this would be the entryway, and there should be a door across from her.

This was no normal house.

There was no telling how it was configured, but wasting time trying to figure out something she had no way of knowing was futile. Instead, she rushed to the sitting room that she had been to before, remembering there was a door on the other side of the room.

Lucy no longer played it safe, deciding that moving slowly and peering around each doorway was simply a luxury that she didn't have time for. Caution was worthless.

Through the door, she found a library. Each wall was covered with floor to ceiling bookcases, packed with old volumes. Books that she was sure would never be touched by Edward, and probably hadn't been by anyone in a century; books lost to time. Under normal circumstances, she would relish the chance to spend time in that room; to flip through book after book, searching for literary treasure. Instead, she ran as fast as she could to the only other door in the room, and opened it.

Another long hallway greeted her. Green carpet ran the length, and the walls were covered with more ridiculously large paintings of people long dead. She turned left, running to the furthest door on the left-hand side of the hallway. She paused as her head began to spin out of control. Her heart had not slowed and she was on the verge of collapse. She wanted to sit, regain her strength, and think. She had run so far and knew that if she had to find her way back, she couldn't. Edward's insanity was mirrored by the walls he had built to contain it.

Move forward or die now.

She tried the knob, and at first thought the door was locked. There were other doors to try, but this one felt right to her, so she turned harder. After enough pressure, there was a loud splintering sound and the knob turned. She released it as the door slowly opened of its own accord. The room opened to her was pitch black. The dark scared her so deeply and she nearly turned around.

Forward!

She ran into the corner of some sort of table almost immediately after entering the room. The glow from the hallway did very little to light her way. After several more bumps and toes crushed from kicking metal, she was able to find a light switch.

Fluorescent bulbs turned on above, humming softly, brightening with the passing moments. She had found the kitchen—the real one. Everything was stainless steel and looked industrial. This was the kind of kitchen designed to serve an army.

Who gives a shit? Keep going.

There were two doors in the kitchen, one straight ahead from the door she had entered by, and another to her right. Lucy chose the right. On the way to the door, she had to brace herself on the countertops, her eyes darkening. She willed herself to go on, and just as Lucy reached the door, she fell forward. She remained there for a moment, vision blurred and spinning. She thought of her father, and decided that even he couldn't expect much more from her under the circumstances.

If nothing else, she had to see what was on the other side of the door. If it was freedom, she may find some extra energy. If it was just another room in this shitty house, then she would lay down and let herself drift away.

She gripped the handle, using it to push her body upright. She took a deep breath as she pulled open the door.

She fell to her knees, knowing that it was all over now.

Another hallway.

Another hallway with Edward Wolcroft leaning against the wall. Todd and her father flanked him on either side. They both had blank faces, as if what was happening to her was inevitable and they had nothing more to feel about it. Oblivious to their presence, Edward stepped forward just as Lucy collapsed into the floor completely.

"Hello, Mother," he said.

PART 2
RELEASE

CHAPTER 1

Her dreams were incandescent paintings of putrification. Her father, impaled with a spear of Lucy's own carving. Her ex-husband, decapitated by a knife wielded with furious precision. The two men that taught her the lessons of life; murdered, so that her mind could survive.

Lucy awoke with a straw in her mouth and the sweet taste of pure water on her tongue. She sucked the fluids down, not questioning from whence they came. Her body was soft molding clay, discerning her current state of being was a chore that she could not undertake.

"Drink as much as you need. There is food too," a voice said from far away. "You have much to do, you will need your strength."

Her eyes were open, but they couldn't see. Colors splashed against her vision, distorted and incomprehensible. She became aware of her hands; untethered. Moving them, she found that she was not devoid of the capability. The color of her hand skid across her eyes, mixing with the rest.

"Are you Edward?"

"Yes," the voice said.

"Which one?"

"I don't know what you mean, mother."

Asked and answered.

At the pace of dripping molasses on a cold day, her vision cleared. She had not been moved. The place of her collapse was the place that she now lay, half of her body in the hall, half in the kitchen. She still could not see Edward.

Get up. At least in a sitting position. Little steps.

Finding the right buttons to click to get each of her parts to co-operate was a task gigantic. Each section of her body seemed to operate on its own set of arbitrary rules and establishing an accord between them was a supreme act of will. She found herself sitting upright as her eyes cleared enough to see the man standing in the hallway, smiling.

"I am glad to see that you are ok. I was awfully worried there for a bit," he said.

"If this is your definition of ok, then you are more delusional than I thought."

"I want to show you something."

"Fuck off," she said, bluntly.

Rather than argue, Edward walked to her, reached down, and deftly pulled Lucy to her feet. She would have collapsed in a heap if he hadn't held her up. He attempted to let her walk, but when it was obviously out of the realm of possibility, he dragged her down the hall and propped her up against a window.

"Take a look," Edward said, excitedly.

Lucy rolled herself over on the window, propping herself up with her hands the best she could. A heavenly light, brighter than she had ever seen, flooded her senses. A welcome wash of white took over her, and for a moment she was in a purgatorial state. To her great distress, the light subsided a little, then more, eventually revealing itself as nothing more otherworldly than the afternoon sun.

The city was vast and illuminated, but it was the swathe of green in the distance that reminded Lucy of home. The trees so numerous that they appeared as one from this distance. She could feel them pulling at her.

"Look down."

She didn't want to look anywhere else. This was her place now, a simple life of staring into an expanse of trees in the distance. Anything was better than following another order from him.

When he saw that she did not comply, Edward tugged on the little lock on the back of her neck and said, "Remember your collar." She did look down then, but not out of the window. Talk of her collar made her remember another unfortunate circumstance - she was still nude. Her heart jumped into full gear at the thought, the world that seemed so fuzzy and out of reach was all at once right in front of her in high definition. Lucy began to panic as she attempted to cover herself from Edward's perverted eyes.

"Please mother, it is far too late for shame. Just look down."

Unwilling to simply let the man ogle her, even though her attempts at coverage were woefully inadequate, she requested that he turn from her. When he seemed to not hear, she relented, and looked back out the window. The sun still shined brightly, but her eyes had almost fully adjusted now. She hadn't noticed before, but the window actually angled outward, and she was able to see all the way to the ground.

Vertigo had never been an issue before for Lucy, but her current state of health caused the dizziness to overtake her. The ground seemed to be rushing up at her like a charging bull. Then, just as suddenly as it had set in, the feeling was gone. She could still feel her heart racing from the fright, but the ground no longer seemed bent on trampling her.

Then, she finally saw what Edward had been trying to get her to see. There were hundreds of people, tiny from this height, flooding out of the building. They all left through the same revolving door and then fanned out in all directions. More and more and more.

"There are so many," Lucy said. "Where are they going? Is something wrong with the building?"

"Not at all. I simply told them to leave."

"Why would you do that?"

"To be alone, of course," he said, grinning. "Thirty six hundred people working in my building, and I doubt a single one would ever dare to come up here. All the same, I didn't want to risk it."

Edward leaned back against the window. He set his head down on the glass and looked completely comfortable; giddy even.

He wants you to see how powerful he is. He wants his 'mother' to be proud.

"I'm impressed," she said, as convincingly as possible. Though, truth was, it was a pretty impressive sight.

"Do you mean it?"

"Yeah."

"Thank you so much! I just wanted you to realize that I was doing a good job. People listen to me now, mom."

She wanted to strangle the life out of him so badly. If she had possessed the strength, she would jump on him right now. Even if he shocked the life out of her, she would take him along for the ride. But she didn't have enough stamina left to crush a beetle. Lucy rolled over, and her body slid down the glass, her ass plopping to the carpeted hallway floor.

"Now what?" she asked. "You take me back to the table. I watch you do some filing. Maybe you kill another hooker while I try and think of pretty things."

"No, mother. Now is the time for you to explore what I have created. I want you to experience everything I have built here. Everything. I have work to do, so I trust you will be ok alone."

What?

"Yes?" she asked, wondering what the right answer was.

"Good, there are clothes for you in that room there," Edward said, pointing to a closed door. "There is some food and water too. Ok?"

"Uh, ok."

"Good! I really hope you like what I've made. I did it all for you."

The sun had nearly deserted the sky entirely before Lucy found the strength and nerve to pick herself up. Edward had not returned in that time, and she didn't have an educated guess as to where he might be. She was no longer in a house; that was obvious. These corridors were typical office fare. Tan carpet, calming blue wall, with cheap prints of paintings that were never that great to begin with.

Straight in front of her was a hallway extending for what seemed like a mile, mocking logical perspective. To her right was a similar hall, but that one ended abruptly a hundred yards away at a large off-white, heavy looking door. The room that Edward had said contained clothes and food was the second on the left going forward, but she went right to inspect the door at the end first. Locked. There were small windows in the door, and she peered through. The glass was distorted, but moving her face into the right angle, she was able to see a sign marking a stairwell. She also could see something dark on the stairway door, but could not make out what it was.

Lucy returned to the hallway junction, and just for the hell of it, she tried the door that led back to the kitchen. It was locked. She found herself thrilled that the door would not open, all too happy to leave Edward's home behind her.

The door that Edward pointed out to her opened into a small closet with nothing inside, except a white t-shirt and a pair of dark blue pants, both hung from hangers, free of wrinkles. On the floor was a carefully folded set of underwear, the same that she had worn the day of her kidnapping, now cleaned. Beside them were three protein bars, a gallon of water, and bandages.

Lucy looked down at her hand and immediately screamed in pain. She was so damaged that her mind had instinctually blocked out the pain she had inflicted on herself but now that she could see the mess she was no longer blissfully ignorant. She wrapped her poor hand in the bandages and did her best to forget about it again.

She dressed quickly, thinking that this was all a mirage that would dissipate; making her once again tied, naked, and bloody. Once fully clothed, she woofed down one bar, stashing the other two in her jeans; one in each pocket. She drank a quarter of the water and opted to use her one good hand to carry the rest of the jug with her, though she didn't yet know where she was going.

Forward is the only way.

With one unsure step after another she made her way down the hall, deciding to pass by all the doors and discover what lay at the end. As Lucy approached the final destination, a sign came into view that made her hasten her step despite the pain.

EXIT.

The word, ELEVATOR, gave her a burst of improbable energy. The sight of the metal mechanical sliding doors was enough to make her forget the pain in her hand. Then, the tiny green light in the center of the elevator buttons gave her hope.

Lucy must have pushed the button enough times to call a freight elevator from Heaven, but nothing happened. The doors never parted. The area around her had a few silk plants and a small table. There was a chair against the wall, and Lucy sank into it, letting the water jug drop to the floor.

Her eyes threatened tears; her body promised collapse.

"Well, you certainly can't go that way," Edward's voice said in a cacophonous roar. His words zig-zagged down the hall, rattling her teeth. "If you leave, you won't see all the surprises I have for you."

He was on a loudspeaker, his voice omniscient, which probably matched his own self-image. The all-powerful being that recreates his past in his own image, and destroys those that turn from him.

You are being watched. He warned you, remember?

"There are many doors back the way you came. Why not try them out?" He laughed into whatever unholy microphone he was speaking through, and the noise clattered through the building with industrial insanity. "I can't wait! I really can't. You are going to be so proud of me!"

His final words echoed through the corridor and split her thoughts in two; one half wanting to discover, the other, needing to recede into the immaterial. She no longer longed for her father's words to help her along, but they were always inside her. Everything he had ever taught her had formed her very soul; leaving only one option.

The red on white letters of the exit sign laughed at her as she stood and turned to face the hallway once more. The distance seemed shorter from this end, perhaps because she already knew what lay at the end.

The first door on the right was locked, as was the one directly across the hall. When Lucy tried the next set, the result was the same. So, when the knob turned on the third door on the left, she flinched, suddenly terrified. The hallway now seemed like the only safe place to be. Whatever crept behind the door was going to hurt her, of that she was sure.

She thought back to all the times that she had hidden in her own home, hoping that Todd wouldn't find her. All the times that she should have stood up and faced him, no matter the beating that may have followed. He was not her ruler, and neither was Edward.

Open the door.

The light in the room was scarlet. Two red bulbs dangled from the ceiling on precariously hung cords. First orange, now red; if she were watching a movie, she would probably scoff at the garishly dramatic decor. *Red; ooooooo spooky.* In reality, it scared the shit out of her.

Scattered around the room were some fake candles exactly the same as those that she had noticed in the dining room, the light they emitted not powerful enough to overcome the redness. Lucy took a couple of steps through the doorway, and as she released the handle, the door slammed shut. Lucy practically leapt in the air, then giggled at the ridiculousness of it all. When she tried the knob again, the door was locked.

Of course.

"Edward, your haunted house bullshit is getting old!"

There was no answer, but she hadn't expected one. Even if he was listening, and she assumed he was, he would never have responded. He only speaks to his mother after all. Lucinda, the woman he kidnapped from a cushy popcorn job, was without a voice.

"Yeah, don't worry. I'm getting rather used to talking to myself," she said to the room.

Even with the red light, the room was remarkably dark. The shadows created by the crimson hue tricked her mind, and the flicker of the fake candlelight gave the room false movement. The right side of the room was more brightly lit than the left, and there was a table there. Upon the table sat a large incense burner with smoke gently rising from a stick of patchouli. She had hated the smell her entire life, reminding her of the strangeness of people. She always thought it to be a scent that only the odd would appreciate.

Sprinkled around the burner were wilted roses, almost black in color, petals wrinkled and curled like an old witch's fingertips. Tipped over on its side was a statue of a nude woman, draped in strategically placed cloth. Her arm was snapped off, lying among the decrepit petals. At the edge of the table was an old shoebox, battered and moldy.

On the wall above the strange shrine were framed photographs, lovingly placed in a circular pattern. Each photo was of the woman that Lucy knew had to be the actual mother of Edward Wolcroft. She was enchantingly beautiful in each photo. Washing dishes, at a family picnic, standing next to an ancient automobile; stunning in them all. She was a woman that would have made every man's head turn, while demanding their respect.

The kind of woman that queens and first ladies were made of.

In the middle of the circle, was a crucifix turned upside down, covered in what Lucy hoped wasn't blood, but knew probably was.

Lucy tried to imagine what Edward did when he stood where she was right now, looking upon his mother's image. He was obsessed, but that was already apparent. What did a person need a shrine for? Was it for love or worship? And the cross, did he follow Satan, or simply denounce God?

She pulled the shoebox into the center of the table, the sides bending, ready to disintegrate. A strange residue rubbed off on her fingers, blackening the tips. Removing the lid of the box was like peeling back cellophane on a TV dinner, but instead of inferior food, she discovered more photos. These did not have the beauty found on the wall.

Lucy turned her back to the box and stared into the dark wall across the way. There was no light in that part of the room, and she saw a blank spot in time inviting her over. She had only seen the photo on the top, but she couldn't look again. She couldn't.

You have to.

You have to.

You have...OK!

The image was of the same beautiful woman she had admired, now lying naked in a bed, her legs spread eagle, and her eyes closed. The photo was old with yellowing edges, and obviously taken by an amateur. She removed the picture and placed it upside down on the table, but the next one was worse. Edward's mother was in the same position, but this one was closer up. The next was completely zoomed in on her crotch.

The series continued as Lucy flipped the photos as quickly as she could. A hand entered the photos, moving the body around into different positions, and groping at her. The photographer rolled her over on her back and then took several of just the woman's face. She didn't appear dead to Lucy, so that was a blessing. She was sleeping, or more likely drugged; perhaps with the same chemicals used on Lucy.

The photos moved down her body, eventually revealing an erect penis hovering above the woman's torso. After the next photo, she couldn't continue. She replaced the damp shoebox lid and began to tear up. She never saw Edward in the pictures, but she knew it was him. It had to be; this was *his* shrine.

Was this all a fantasy for him? Did he kidnap her and Roger to live out what he wished he had done as a boy, or was he recreating exactly what had already happened?

With both palms on the table, she leaned over and let herself cry. Her stomach felt as if it would evacuate its contents, but she knew she couldn't afford to lose the nutrition and willed it to settle. She squeezed her eyes tight and kept them there until there was a sudden clicking sound and a bright glow against the wall, casting her shadow across the crucifix.

Lucy didn't turn around right away, too frightened of what she might find, choosing instead to ignore the danger. Maybe her death would come quick, and without her knowledge.

Easy.

The sounds of movement behind her sounded ethereal, as if they weren't really there at all. She kept waiting for the ominous creator of the noise to attack, yet she remained untouched. It was one spoken word that forced her to turn.

"Mother."

Edward's voice sent her into an immediate frenzy, the disgusting photographs burned into her anger. The man would pay.

But, Edward was not there. No one was. Instead, there were television monitors. Nine of them, arranged into a perfect grid that covered the majority of the far wall. What had been a primordial black was now bright with images of herself lying motionless on a bed. The same bed that Edward had brought her to; where he had raped her.

"Mother," Edward said again. The audio on the video wasn't the best, but his voice was unmistakable. Lucy was wearing the blue dress, pulled down to her waist.

The camera approached her, then wobbled as Edward climbed onto the bed. Lucy watched as he touched her. Squeezing and teasing her flesh. Pulling the clothes that he had forced her to wear down to her feet, before tossing them off camera.

He zoomed in to her face in the same way that he had with his true mother. Lucy found her own face troubling. Why wasn't she waking up? How could she have let him do this to her? Drugged or not, it was no excuse! She almost believed that the Lucy on screen deserved what was coming. She hadn't acted when she should have. She hadn't fought when there was still time to fight. That Lucy had destroyed her.

This Lucy couldn't watch. She clenched her eyes, vowing to never open them again. The sounds still echoed softly in the room and she tried to cover her ears. Covering the right was easy, but her broken hand made it difficult to block the sound from her left.

This pain is everything.
This pain is all I have.

The glow pulsed on the other side of her eyelids. It would stop soon. It had to.

"Don't you want to see?" Edward asked. The voice boomed, and it was not a part of the video. She dropped her aching palm from her left ear. "This is proof of our love, mother. You and I were meant to be together. This is the evidence. I knew you needed convincing, so I thought I would show you. Why aren't you watching?"

"No! I am not watching your filth. You raped her!"

He didn't hear Lucy, and he never would. She had to make him listen, and the only voice he heard was that of this mother.

"Edward. My s...son. Listen to me. I don't need to see this." Her voice trembled in tiny earthquakes. "I love you. Ok? I realize it now, so you can let me go. I don't need to see this."

"You don't want to see?" Edward asked.

"Maybe later."

Oh damnit, I'm losing it!

"I mean, of course I do, but right now I want to see what else you have made for me."

Seconds.

Ticked.

By.

Then the video stopped, and the room went dark again, followed by the sound of unlocking doors.

Lucy choked on her relief, coughing vigorously.

CHAPTER 2

Every time a path was opened for Lucy, she grew wearier. How long would this last? How long could *she* last? She should have been happy that the door unlocked and she was able to leave the horrifying red room, but tasking herself to move wasn't easy. Every part of her body had a pain; every part of her mind, a hole.

Even as she was considering her health and will, her hand was on the doorknob. There was a region somewhere in her brain that was operating independently of the rest of her. The chunk that was still controlled by her father.

The door opened to another hallway, identical to the previous one except for the blood smeared on the wall directly across from Lucy. It started as just a few small streaks, but the blood was a trail that became denser the further along the hallway it went. Lucy looked to the right and followed the vermillion road with her eyes, like a bloody arrow leading her.

She took her steps slowly, never looking away from the blood on the wall. It grew thicker, and was still wet. In parts, it shined in the light, and Lucy was tempted to reach out and run her fingers through the fluid. In a few more steps, the pure liquidity of it changed, now becoming chunky. Small pieces of gelatinous mush, getting larger with every step she took.

The chunks resembled raw hamburger meat, freshly ground and plastered. The smell of it got deeper and more pronounced. Before long, Lucy was able to make out actual shapes in the gore, fleshy hunks that used to be a part of a person. Fingernail fragments, large segments of stretched skin, bloody tufts of hair stuck in piles of human grime.

At last, she reached the end of the line. She was at the door she had previously seen through the distorted window. The door to the stairs, with the indiscernible dark thing on the front. The thing that turned out to be Roger's face, peeled from his skull, and tacked up like a poster on a dorm room wall.

Lucy wanted to get upset, scared, but the most she could manage was apathy. Roger had violated her, and even if it wasn't completely his doing; she still hated him. She just couldn't help it. Staring at his face now was like confronting an old foe. They were in the same game but he had already lost.

She pushed the door open, careful not to touch anything unseemly, and began to ascend the stairs, leaving Roger behind to think about what he had done.

One flight down, Lucy tried the door with the large, green number 54, and found it locked. Another flight, and 53 disappointed her too.

52.

51.

50.

That was the end of the line. Instead of stairs to the 49th floor, there was only a wall to bang her head against. She sat down on the final step, winded and dejected. Just going down the stairs had been trying for her and now she would have to go back up. It seemed impossible.

That was when Lucy realized that she had forgotten the jug of water back at the useless elevator. It would still be complacently sitting there next to the chair, and her mistake might prove costly. Lucy looked behind at the rising steps, counting them. Just a single flight would take her twenty grueling lifts of her broken body. It couldn't be done.

You can make it, or die trying. Either way, you win.

Balancing herself on the handrail, Lucy pulled her body up. She put pressure on her injured hand, but the pain there just blended with all the rest. Each time she raised her foot to take the next step, she counted as she pressed down and forced her body higher. Twenty became ten, five, and then she was back to floor 51.

As her mind celebrated, her body collapsed, and it was some time before she was able to face the journey to 52. During the wait, she consumed one of the protein bars, hoping for a jolt of energy, but getting a stomach ache instead.

Halfway up the next flight, Lucy left some of the food in a sticky pile on step number sixteen. It looked like discarded oatmeal from a disgruntled child. She kept going.

As she stepped on the landing of 54, she was too dizzy to keep her eyes open, and her heart had beat so fast that she lost it long ago. She didn't need eyes to climb, but if her equilibrium failed her, she would be done. She heard footsteps behind her, clomping down heavily on the steps behind her, echoing against the solid walls. Lucy turned to watch but hadn't the energy to brace herself for who she might see.

The footsteps thumped on, one after another, never sounding any closer. Step. Step. Step.

Whoever it was would have gotten to her by now. They would be looking her straight in the face, yet there was no one at all. Just the steps. Whoever it was, they weren't going to show themselves, but they had the right idea. She had steps to take. Only one more flight.

Twenty.

Eleven.

Four.

55.

When at last she had reached the beginning again, she rejoiced, collapsed, and fell asleep to the sound of endless phantom footsteps.

Time was meaningless now, so it didn't matter how long she was passed out and she made no attempt to guess. Lucy gathered her wits, liquid as they were. She didn't feel any better, but she had gotten some energy back. It was useless to stay on floor 55, she would need to go up.

She took the steps more easily than she anticipated. At the final step, she began to pray. Not to a god so much as the universe. *Please. Please. Let the door open.*

The universe answered in the affirmative, and the door pushed open then slammed itself closed behind her. The crashing sound reverberated through the hall in front of her. Another empty hall that seemed to extend into the next life, lined with doors that seemed inviting, but would most certainly pull the football out of the way just before she kicked.

Even so, Lucy tried the first door on the left.

Locked.

The next. Locked.

Locked.

Locked.

Each door tried, and each unwilling to give up its contents, until the very last. Anxious to see the other side, even knowing that there couldn't be anything good, she pushed the door wide.

On the opposite side was nothing but another hallway, identical to the one she was in. Lucy walked through the door and stared down the new corridor. All of the doors on the right-hand side just connected to this one.

"What the fuck is wrong with this fucking place!" Lucy yelled. "God dammit Edward, what the hell do you want?"

"I built it for you mother," the loudspeaker Edward said.

"I don't want it! It doesn't even make sense!"

"Aren't you amazed at what I've done?"

"No! You've made me open doors and climb stairs for hours. The only thing I am ever going to find is more of your games."

"You don't like the doors? I can help."

Immediately, every door in the hallway opened except the one right in front of her.

"Those are empty. Now you can move on. All you have to do is ask, mother. I want you to be happy. Go see what I left you."

The door had a small note attached to it that she had not noticed before. She had to squint just to make out the words.

You probably don't want to go in here,
but you don't really have a choice, do you?

The knob did indeed turn, and as she cracked the door, Lucy heard a sound like a motor chugging along. The sound was like a small car that was having an enormously hard time driving up a mountainside. The room was pitch black.

Lucy inched around the room with her hand against the wall, searching for a switch. The noise grew a little louder as she went on, and now she could hear a wet sound attached to it. The small car splashing in the rain. Still, she couldn't find a switch, so doubled back and began to search on the opposite wall.

When she finally found the light switch, Lucy was ecstatic, every small victory now a major event in her new life. She managed a smile, though when she turned to view the room, her smile hardened into place, unable to grow or shrink. She stood frozen in place, unable to fully justify what she was see-ing. When she screamed, she was unaware. When she vomited bile down her chest, she remained oblivious. The scene before her had ended comprehension.

Bonnie, the secretary with the crotch of gold, was on a table. Her body was naked, tied in place by barbed wire twisted around each wrist that extended to bolts on each wall. Her mouth was gaping wide with old blood caked around her mouth, and her skin was light blue; veins dark like tree branches in the fog.

Bonnie's legs were spread wide, also with barbed wire holding them in place, and nearly pure white. They shook as the motor turned. Her body animated, though dead.

The motor turned and turned, spinning the piston pointed into Bonnie's crotch. The piston moved back and forth, resisting each time. On the end of the piston was a large black penis, rubber, or whatever they made those dildos out of. Fastened in the three places around the fake phallus with more barbed wire were three large kitchen knives, completely covered and dripping with flesh and particles of bone.

As the knives stabbed into the woman, the wet noise drowned Lucy's ears, and she tried without luck to find a way to stop the motor's ceaseless penetration. The assistant's femininity was no longer discernable, now just a ground pile of meat for the knives to eviscerate. The woman's blood still dripped from her body in places, but much had coagulated and now just lingered, darkening.

Pieces of Bonnie were pulled from the pile and discarded on the floor as the motor continued to drill the psycho-sexual apparatus into the woman. Lucy watched as the small chunks fell to the floor, joining the rest that had fallen before she had gotten there. She was going to be sick again. And again. She would never be well.

"Horrible, isn't it," Edward said from the door. "He's got a sick sense of humor."

Lucy sat on the floor and watched the parts of Bonnie the secretary plunge to the floor.

Edward leaned against the doorway, the cherry on his cigarette shining bright as he took a drag. Lucy didn't' want to acknowledge him. Good Edward, bad Edward; she no longer cared. It was his hands that did this to Bonnie; that smeared Roger on the wall.

Fucking Roger.

She held her hands as tight against her ears as she could, still watching the floor. She didn't see as Edward walked over to the machine and pressed a button that she never found. The motor slowed, shrieking in happiness that its labor was finally done. The wet sounds stopped, yet Lucy swore she could still hear them.

Lowering her hands, she saw Edward walk over to her. She had a fleeting desire for reaction, but ignored it. What was in store for her? Would it be as bad as what happened to Bonnie? Worse?

He sat down on the floor, crisscross-applesauce, and waited for Lucy to acknowledge him. He lit another cigarette. Lucy looked up and was grateful that the man's head blocked the majority of the horror show behind.

"Back again, huh?" she said.

"It would seem so. I didn't think I would be."

"Why are you here?"

"No idea."

Lucy reached her hand out to him.

"Give me one of those?"

"You smoke?" he asked.

"Not until right now. Not much reason not to anymore. May as well try it."

Edward pulled another cigarette and tossed it into his mouth, deftly catching it between his lips right next to the one he already had. He took the lit cigarette and pushed it into the tip of the new one, inhaling. He handed the cigarette over, and Lucy fumbled the pass, dropping it to the floor and watching it roll away. She leaned over and grabbed it, put it in her mouth, and inhaled.

The coughing lasted for a while, but when she got it together, she tried again.

"Not so much this time," Edward said.

Lucy did as instructed and inhaled just slightly. The smoke filling her lungs burned, but was still pleasant somehow. As she exhaled, her head became light, and her eyes started to flutter and roll back. She managed to catch herself from passing out again, but she took her time before taking another drag.

"Where do you think you'll go now?" Edward asked.

"Wherever you lead me, I guess."

"I would tell you if I knew. I want you to get out. I never really cared about the others."

"The others?"

"Sure, you aren't the first. Hopefully you will be last though. Like I said, they are closing in. I doubt I will be free much longer."

Lucy took several more drags, already an old pro. Her head stayed light, but she was enjoying it. This Edward had a soothing quality on her. It helped that she knew she was safe until he changed back. It was the only time she could really slow down without fear.

"Tell me about this place," she said.

"I told you before, it's a company. I run a lot from here, have a lot of money and power. I'm getting tired of it though."

"I mean, tell me about the building. Do you know why the house was built? Do you know what this whole setup is about?"

Edward lit another cigarette.

"I don't know that much. My father built the building. I inherited it. At some point, the top eight floors were cut off."

"Cut off?"

"The offices only go up to the 49th floor now. The rest is all his. I generally stick to the office and work. Sometimes I find myself in other places, and I deal with it."

"You don't ever remember being the other Edward?"

"I blank it out I think. I know that he remembers me though. I don't know for sure, but I think I am around less and less. It's all very confusing. That's why I can't help you. I don't know what would happen to me if I did."

They both finished their cigarettes and put them out on the floor. He asked Lucy if she would like another, but she waved him off. Once was enough, and she was feeling sick again.

Lucy pointed behind Edward and said, "You aren't bothered by that?"

"Honestly?"

"Yeah."

"It doesn't really bother me anymore," he said, looking back at what was left of Bonnie. "That one is pretty gross though."

"Gross may be an understatement."

"I've seen a lot. Might as well just be horror movie effects now. Same difference."

"You know," she said, "I was married once."

"Yeah, what happened?"

"I killed him."

"He deserve it?"

"Yes, and so do you. I plan to kill you too, Edward."

He stood up and dropped a cigarette down to the floor in front of her. "Just in case you change your mind," he said, then walked back to the doorway. "You won't see me again. I'm sure of it this time."

"Ok."

He turned to leave, but stopped short.

157

"I do hope you manage to kill me, Lucinda. Good luck."

Alone again.

CHAPTER 3

The round table was not one she recognized, but Lucy felt comfortable at it. Wherever she was, it was dark, with only the table and its occupants visible. Her father sat across from her, stoic and harsh. Todd sat between them, creating a perfect triangle. His face was smashed up and entirely red with blood, seeming more like a freshly peeled tomato than a human being. Lucy looked at her father, who looked at Todd, who looked at her.

At the center of the table sat a gun, perpetually spinning clockwise. The gun fired, but the bullet passed harmlessly between Todd and her father. The bang was not as loud as it should have been, the surrounding darkness devoured the sound.

Todd was the first to speak. "I didn't deserve this."

Lucy laughed, still looking at her father.

"You deserved way more than what you got." she said. "Why did you leave, daddy?"

"I already told you why." her father said. The gun went off again, this time sending a bullet slicing across her father's arm, though he took no notice of it. He began to bleed into sleeve of his shirt. "I told you all of it. Why did you beat my little girl?"

"I never did anything that she didn't ask for. She was always fucking with me. Always acting like she was superior," Todd said, never looking away from Lucy. "I may have drunk too much sometimes, but did that mean I had to die?"

"I'm only sorry that I didn't leave the first time you hit me. I believed your lies for too many years. If I could go back, I would kill you directly, instead of just letting you die." Another bullet shot out, but only struck the dark. "What was it – twelve years later that you explained yourself, daddy? I was in college. I could have used you before then. Maybe if you had stuck around, I wouldn't be where I am now."

"You didn't need me then, and you don't need me now. You never needed me." Her father turned to look at her. "I didn't teach you anything that you couldn't have learned yourself."

Lucy turned her head, looking out into the black space between her father and ex-husband. The gun kept spinning and spinning. The two men began to berate her.

"I didn't deserve to die."

"Just forget me."

"Why would you kill me?"

"Forget everything I taught you."

"I promise that I will never hit you again."

"I can't deal with this anymore."

Lucy reached forward and slammed her hand down on the gun, the grip spinning perfectly into her hand. She raised the gun and pointed it at Todd; right between the eyes. She pulled the trigger and as the bullet pierced his skull, his body evaporated. Lucy then turned the gun on her father, who smiled back at her.

"That's right," he said.

She shot him and watched the mist of his body sink into the dark.

The gray matter of Lucy's brain felt like it was ready to be packed and sold for pig feed. Before opening her eyes, she tried again to calculate how many days she had been captive, but that number was unattainable. A week? Two?

It couldn't be two.

You have no idea what it could be. Just open your eyes.

She was horizontal and didn't even know it, unable to feel the hard floor against her face; her body just one big hurt. The mound of Bonnie's parts had drained a trickle of blood that zig-zagged through the tile grit, nearly making it all the way to Lucy's face. The crimson pathway had coagulated and darkened before it could reach her. She shifted her eyeballs upward to see the table that Bonnie's corpse lay, hoping that it would be gone; miracled away into the grand design.

The mutilated pile of dead flesh was still there, but the angle that Lucy lay didn't give her a clear view, or the best view, depending on what you were looking for. She looked at the barbed wire restrained right arm to see that Bonnie wore a silver ring with a large green jewel. Costume jewelry to be sure, but the stone still caught the light. Lucy focused on the sparkle, even as the rest of her vision blurred, erasing the room around her and her thoughts of the dead woman with it.

The sweet taste of sleep didn't quite come to her this time, and Lucy was forced to move her dilapidated body and face onward to the next big thing. The next task that Edward had for her. The next display of death to admire. Cringing as she rose, Lucy could hear the bones crack and grind in her back. Her feet, and most of her right leg were numb, starting to prickle as her body allowed blood flow to return. Her mouth was a desert, and she lamented the bottle of water; her only oasis.

Leave the room. Don't look at the body. Don't look at the machine. He said there were 57 floors. There is still one to check.

Getting to her feet was easier if she did it with her eyes closed. That was something to remember. Managing to curb the morbid desire to look back to the body, she made it to the door and was back out into the hallway with the horror safely contained behind her. After passing through the door in front of her, stepping into the adjoining hallway, Lucy trip-walked to the stairway door, groaning every other step. She felt two hundred years young.

The first ten steps up to the midway landing point took more energy than she knew she possessed, but once on the landing, pointing herself toward the second ten, Lucy saw something that gave her total pause.

The walls were painted with erotic images, like those found in the Kama Sutra, yet painted with the hand of a five-year-old. Quick lines, blurred colors, and haphazard detail created pictures of deviant sex and murder. Blood was depicted as splatters of Crayola red. Straight line penises entered winking eye vaginas. Each juvenile rendition bloodier than the next and more depraved as she climbed the steps. In one, the spiral anus of a woman was being ripped by a devil's pitchfork. Another had two men pulling a woman's body apart, her waist spilling onto the ground; their comically rendered cocks ejaculating milky white semen onto spaghetti-like intestine.

At the top of the stairs, Lucy was ready to move on but the door to floor 57 rejected her. The artist had somehow made the large green numbers into two men engaged in carnal pleasures above a pool of blood without origin.

Another locked door. The game was rigged; the deck was stacked.

The realization reminded Lucy's body of its limits, and she sat on the top step, analyzing all that she could see.

It didn't make sense.

Edward was crazy, but he was meticulous. Each new horror he had shown her was planned and had meaning. These paintings didn't say anything, they simply shocked; and not very well after seeing Bonnie downstairs. Why would he have left these here for her to find? There was no story here. This was not something that would impress a mother.

Are you seriously still trying to figure him out? Who cares why he painted them. Maybe he liked to come up here and jerk off before board meetings. What does it matter?

It matters.

I think.

She finally had time to sit with her thoughts, but she was unable to maintain any thought process for long. Her vision blurred and spun as the effort of the climb took its piece of what was left of her. She couldn't stop, but oh how she longed to! Her father wouldn't let her, and he never would. His mind was in hers. He had placed it within her when she was a young, naïve child, desperate for knowledge. It was only knowledge that he had and it doomed her to a life of desperately clawing forward through time when her universe clearly wanted her to give in to gravity and collapse.

Grasping tightly to the hand rail, Lucy pulled her body up-right and descended the stairs back to floor 56. There was nowhere else to go, and nothing to hope for other than a new unlocked door back where she started. Hope was unnecessary, she thought. Edward would lead her.

She left the paintings, and all the confusion they inspired sitting next to door 57.

Two paths were open to Lucy, and though it wasn't a difficult choice, she was having a hard time making a move.

Left, or right?

Such a simple choice, yet completely debilitating. To the left, she had the door with the blurry window that would lead her back to the kitchen. To the right, a long hallway that she had already traversed, but may have newly opened doors. It didn't matter which way she went, and Lucy knew it. There was no way to tell the correct course of action, yet she was paralyzed with indecision.

Her thoughts floated behind her eyes, and not a single one would sit still long enough for her to make a decision. She had gotten light headed going down the stairs and had to stop twice to catch her breath. Now, she stood just outside the stairway door, Roger's peeled face inches from kissing the back of her neck.

Left, or right?

Lucy grasped at comprehension, trying desperately to put ideas in a row. She stared down the lengthy hallway to the right, focusing on each door, but they ran together, becoming one single entryway to the unknown. Her father stood at the end of the hall. No, not the end. The end was out of sight. He was much closer to Lucy than she thought, one hand grasping a doorknob. Why was he here now? He didn't speak to her, but she knew that he wanted her to follow him.

Stop it! You're hallucinating you dolt! Your father is dead. Massive heart attack, remember? You didn't make it to the funeral. Snap out of it! You are just dehydrated and weak. Move your body now, because I can't do it for you.

Her father walked away, trying to find the end of the endless hallway, eventually vanishing from sight. Hallucinations had always seemed like an impossibility to her. It was impossible to imagine what it would be like to see something that isn't there so vividly. Lucy regrouped, pulling her mind up from its wading pool, and setting it back on course. She would go right.

The first door was locked, and already she began to think that the mirage of her father had led her astray. The door across the hall was locked also. Her frustrations were piling high, and without truly realizing it, Lucy began to yell at Edward.

"WHERE THE HELL DO I GO, YOU CRAZY BASTARD?!"

The next door on the right wouldn't open.

"If you don't hurry up and finish this game of yours, I'm going to die. You won't be able to show me anything else when I'm dead."

The crusted, bloody flesh caked to the wall she passed reminded her of red velvet cake batter.

"Oh right, you won't hear me unless I pretend to be your mother. Well fine, I'm your mother now," she said, trying and failing to open the next door on the left. "And, I've got news for you."

The door to the photograph room didn't open either. Nor did the one across the hall.

"Your mother is very disappointed in you. In fact, your mother..."

The next doorknob up the hall turned in her hand. The mechanism made a click, and the door pushed in.

"...hates you," Lucy said in a whisper, taking a step into a brightly lit room.

Her father was there, and he looked pleased with himself. The fluorescent lights hummed above him, and for a time Lucy could see nothing else. His body began to flicker like an old analog television picture with bad reception, and then it was gone. Her father had disappeared like the illusion he was, and maybe that was for the best.

When Lucy had seen Roger beaten to a pulp, her senses had boiled in intense shock. When she found his body smeared along the wall, her stomach had been ready to plunge from her midsection and join him there. The mutilation of Bonnie was something that should have broken her entirely, but instead left her hollow. Now, her capacity to feel appalled was gone. She tried so hard to find that sense of humanity as she gazed upon the body of FBI Agent Henderson. She needed to know that under all the haze, she was still a human being that could wilt at such a sight as this. Instead, she felt very little, having lost most of what made a person react proportionally to phantasmagoric butchery.

Henderson was in a chair in the middle of the room, though Lucy doubted he had sat of his own accord. The chair itself was made of simple, unfinished lumber, and jutting up from each surface were numerous large nails. Henderson's naked body was pushed down into these nails, and his flesh sat pierced and claret. The nails protruded through his forearms, thighs, and groin. The tips of what must have been exceptionally long spikes just barely pushed through his chest and gut. The head was happily devoid of puncture, but still hung slack. Henderson's eyes were open, as was his mouth, but the expression was elastic and devoid of soul.

Was Lucy, too, devoid of a soul? Could a person look upon what she was seeing and have no reaction if they were filled with the essence of a higher power and purpose? She had become a walking shell that carried nothing but a mind unwilling to cooperate; a mind that she no longer felt to be her own. How else could such a mind make decisions, yet not listen to the person to which it belonged?

You are cracking up, Lucinda. Bonkers and broomsticks. You an Edward deserve each other. I am *you. Do you not get that anymore?*

She didn't.

Across Henderson's belly was a long slice, and out of it was pulled his insides. The intestines had been drawn forth and placed neatly on the floor, spelling out a very predictable word. The guts, written in perfect cursive, said, "Mother."

Lucy had never had the insides of a man talk to her directly, even with a case of mistaken identity, but she was too tired to care. Her face was weary; her body more liquid than solid. She wished that her father would return. That she could take his hand, and they could escape to the forest together, never bothering to re-emerge into this world again. This new world; filled with death and decay. Filled with false reality and true torture.

Lucy somehow knew she would never see that forest again except in dreams.

The intestines again said, "Mother," having no idea that Lucy had heard that joke far too many times before.

***

Leaving the unfortunate agent Henderson to simmer in his fate, Lucy walked through the far wall door, and found herself in another familiar hallway. To the left she could return to the kitchen, and to the right she could try her chances with the useless elevator, as well as get her water back.

That choice was a simple one, even for her.

After many uneven steps, Lucy's bottom plopped into the chair, and her hand naturally dangled down to where the water bottle awaited her. Three quarters of a gallon of pure, clear water slid down her throat as Lucy opened her gullet, barely needing to swallow. Her gag reflex must have disappeared alongside her humanity.

She sat in the chair, staring into the void, thinking of nicer times. For some reason, she looked back to a moment with Todd that occurred before his true nature revealed itself. They had just started dating, and Lucy had yet to quit her college life. He surprised her one night, sneaking into her dormitory without getting caught by Gerta Drummer, the hall director from hell. He brought a brown paper bag of goodies that included two joints, a half bottle of rum, condoms, and a VHS copy of *Faces of Death 3*. At the time, Lucy was fascinated by death captured on video. Looking back, those silly tapes weren't shit.

Todd had been sweet the whole night, mostly keeping his hands to himself. They had only recently begun dating, and she hadn't gone all the way with him yet. She knew that he was getting frustrated with her, but she wanted to be sure this time. The last guy she had slept with turned out to be a real creep. After the television turned to snow, and the VCR began to rewind the tape, Todd leaned into her hard, pressing his body close, and began feeling her up. She had politely asked him to stop, but he hadn't, and she had relented. Five minutes later, he was inside her, and a couple minutes later, he was getting dressed to go.

At the time, she thought that she had done the right thing. She chose not to push him away because he had waited long enough. Now, she thought of her young self as a fool. She had no desire to sleep with him that night. She had given in because she thought it was the right thing to do. She couldn't even remember if he had even used one of the condoms from the goodie bag.

You've always been an idiot when it comes to those things.

Lucy was beginning to think that she drank too much water, too fast. Her stomach was making noises akin to night raids in Fallujah, when she suddenly got an intense feeling in her crotch. The water had gone straight through her, and she had to urinate. Now.

Even after everything, it felt wrong to crouch down and piss on the floor, the rules of proper etiquette so ingrained in even the most mangled parts of her.

Just go. You would rather wet yourself than the carpets of a serial killer?

She was right. After unbuttoning her jeans, Lucy dropped them to the floor and tried to bend her knees. Her strength gave out on her halfway through her crouch, and her ass hit the floor. Embarrassed by her own ineptitude, she bent her knees and wrapped her arms around them, then let the urine flow straight into the carpet. Her ass got wet, but it didn't matter. It took all matter of wiggle and squirm to get herself back on her feet, and many more minutes of struggle just to get her pants back up. The moment she refastened the button and looked up into the long hallway, a door on the right; about 20 feet in front of her, opened.

Lucy braced herself for what may be coming through the door, but nothing ever did. Slowly, like a timid mouse longing for trapped cheese, she approached the open door, thinking that any moment, Edward or some ghostly hallucination would jump out at her, giving her the final fright to end the sluggish beating of her heart. She pulled the door fully open, and found no evil, real or imaginary, waiting for her. Just another room, empty save a few plants; silken and dusty, and another elevator. This one with only an up-arrow button to press.

Without hesitation, Lucy reached out to press that button, knowing in her gut that the elevator doors would not part, but unable to banish the hope. Just as her finger grazed the brush metal of the button, she absentmindedly looked up and froze. There was one more door on the opposite wall; unassuming except for a small metal plate to the left of it. A plate with the name that haunted her with every new step.

Edward Wolcroft.

The office.

The same place that she had looked into with disgust for an untold number of days. Where she had watched people fuck and people die. Visions of sharks entered her mind, their circular pattern unforgettable, even with a mind full of muck. Lucy did not push the elevator button, choosing the office instead. Something made her want to see the reality of what she only knew through an orange dream world. She needed to see what truly lay behind the red curtain.

Another little prayer to the universe, and Lucy tried the handle. It clicked and opened. She pulled the door toward her, walking into the room through the same entrance that she had seen Edward leave through many times. The low hum of aquarium pumps was to her right and bright, mid-day sun shone majestically through the window on left. But, it was right in front of her that her attentions were drawn.

She almost passed out.

She almost screamed.

Instead, she sat. Letting her body sink into the same swivel chair that agent Henderson had waited in.

Agent Henderson.

The deceased Agent Henderson.

In front of her, where there should have been a reflection of herself, was a simple window, with orange light easily visible. Her orange light. There was no one-way mirror, just a clear view of Lucy's hellish home away from home. Her table was there, looking cold and uninviting even from here. Surrounding the table stood all of them. All of those people that she had seen mutilated, bloody, and gone.

Agent Henderson was there, his teeth shining in his smile. Bonnie stood to his left, intact and smirking. The hooker killed with the yank of a whip seemed distracted, but alive.

And, Roger.

Roger stood in the same place that he had once been captive, fully whole, and laughing maniacally.

Your mind has finally completely snapped in two, Lucinda. Even I don't know what to...

A hand touched Lucy's shoulder. It was a light touch; one that would instill comfort in any other situation. She looked up into Edward's eyes. He was smiling too, and not in a way that she had ever seen before.

"Let the confusion nestle in, because...oh Lucy, Lucy, Lucy. Dearest Lucinda, this is the very best part."

CHAPTER 4

The candles had been replaced. Where there were once fake plastic tubes with light bulbs screwed in, were now honest to goodness wax and flaming wicks. With everything else, Lucy was fascinated that they would even take the time.

She had thought at first that her hallucinations had grown more elaborate, but when the group of dead people began to clap and laugh, she began to have doubts. Edward had foretold confusion, and in this he was a prophet.

What is happening?

The living phantoms filed out of the orange room, waving at her all the way, and Edward pulled her to her feet. He didn't speak to her – keeping her in the dark was probably the more entertaining option – but led her through the reception room, passing Bonnie's desk, then through another door. From there, they were back in the house, in rooms she had not seen. It was a quick trek to the dining room, where the brightly lit candles cast demonic shadow swirls across the ceiling.

Edward sat Lucy in her usual place. To her left sat Bonnie, who smiled gleefully as she took sips from a heaping glass of red wine. Next to Bonnie, sat Agent Henderson, also imbibing the drink of victory. Across the table sat the prostitute that wasn't, though what she was remained a mystery.

Just across the table from her, sat Roger, grinning. Grinning.

Lucy longed for a reaction to come from herself. Anything at all to prove that she was still a living creature. She should scream. She should fight. Instead, she could only look on as the group made merry, laughing. Laughing.

Edward gave her a look, then took a sip from the glass waiting for him at the head of the table, before exiting through the swinging door. Roger's eyes were locked on her cemented face. The face that could show no more fright; no more surprise. She remembered the look that the young ragamuffin had given her employee at the popcorn shop. The look of lust. Yes, she knew it well.

Where was the voice residing within her? Where was the voice of Lucinda, woman of constant diligence and poise? How was she to comprehend all of this if her own sense had left her?

I'm still here, but I've got nothing. Not a damn thing.

The door flew open as Edward returned, holding a familiar silver tray. This time, the dead bird, cooked golden brown, steamed and sizzled. Just as the candles had been replaced, so too had the food.

Real food.

Edward sat the tray in front of her and pulled a carving knife stashed in his belt. He wasted no time carving the turkey, and Lucy watched as each remarkably juicy slice slowly flopped over, sending smells in her direction that she had never expected to experience again.

The others quieted as they too marveled at the bounty before them, like carrion eaters wise to the recent demise of some unfortunate beast. When he had cut plenty for all, he used the knife and two fingers to place three large slices on Lucy's plate.

"For you, this must be a heavenly sight," he said.

It was. Lucy's mouth watered even though it had sat parched, but she dared not pick up a slice. Did she? Such a ravenous conundrum to eat from the hand that kills you.

"It is quite alright. It's only food. You remember how to eat, don't you?"

Giving in to a deep primal need, she dug into the turkey breast, using no utensil. The juice of the meat smeared her face and filled her hands. Bits of turkey fell from her maw as she inhaled her dinner. Laughter erupted from the table, but Lucy couldn't get herself to stop eating.

"Give her some more!" Henderson snorted.

"Oh yes, I want to see the dirty thing slurp her slop," said Bonnie as she downed the remainder of her drink. She lit a cigarette and poured herself another glass from one of the many bottles that littered the table.

Edward transferred several more slices to her plate. As she raised the meat to her mouth, Roger grabbed a handful of scraps from the carcass and threw it down in front of her, laughing. The bird parts splashed against the plate, some skipping into her chest, yet still she chewed. These people could treat her as they wanted for now, the only thing that mattered was the delicious energy that messily filled her stomach.

Everyone laughed, and Roger took his cue to throw more. Surprisingly, Edward laid his own hand on Roger's as he grabbed for ammunition a third time.

"That is enough, save some for the rest. First, we dine, and then we revel."

Edward left the room again, and even with their leader absent, the others minded their manners. When he returned, he brought with him another large tray with several dishes. Lucy didn't know what each thing was, but the smells blended together into a culinary perfume that she could get quite used to.

One dish was an orange color, smooth and shiny. Another was white and soupy. The third was the largest mound of caviar than Lucy had ever seen. The dinner guests took their turns at each dish, taking appropriate portions with equally appropriate etiquette. As her belly filled, Lucy's embarrassment at her behavior blossomed. Even in the company of psychosis, she felt a need to impress. Grabbing her napkin, she sat up straight, and cleaned herself as best she could, pushing much of the scattered turkey to the floor.

The subtle noises of polite society eating dinner filled the room. Light taps of sterling silverware against fine china. The smallest of burps; muffled by linen napkins. Subtle chewing sounds held in check so as to not appear to be eating at all. Lucy sat motionless and listened to each sound blend with the next.

"Your entire life is a joke to these people."

Lucy couldn't see her father, but she felt his presence behind her. She didn't turn to look.

"Not even a joke," he continued. "You are a footnote to a punchline that will be forgotten in a day. It shames me to see you like this."

Her father's words once again stung when they should have run off her back. He would probably always be able to say just the right thing to make her feel worse than she already did. The only consolation was that he was truly a hallucination, unlike everyone else at the table.

When at last the meal was through, Edward poured himself a fresh glass of wine and stood. Everyone looked in his direction, including Lucy, as he raised his glass. Each of the others raised their own glasses and listened intently.

"To another successful play!" he said, with triumphant enthusiasm. "I believe this was our best showing yet."

"Hear, hear!"

"Absolutely!"

Edward took a rather large gulp and continued, "Each of you played your parts with divine precision."

A thought suddenly occurred to Lucy, and she interrupted without thinking. "What is your real name?"

Edward caught his next words in his mouth and looked down at her, visibly annoyed.

"You may continue to think of me as Edward, for there is no reason for you to know any different. Likewise, for the rest of our company. And, if you feel the need to interrupt these proceedings again, I suggest you hold your tongue, lest I remove it with a dull blade."

Lucy's jaw clamped shut.

"Now, to continue, every person here should be commended. To Magdalena, our lovely whore. There are no small parts. La di da."

In unison, the table said, "Cheers," and took a drink.

"To our letter of the law, Henderson," Edward continued, "He played his part with menace and panache."

"Cheers."

"To our beloved Roger, who took his licks with pride. A consummate professional if there ever was one. Your wounds will heal, but your sacrifices will never be forgotten."

"Cheers!"

"And of course, I do not want to leave out our star. Lucinda. Trash she may be, but more entertaining refuse there has never been. She gave us a few surprises, didn't she?"

The table raised their glasses and took a drink, but there was no chant of glee for her.

"But, it is to Bonnie that we tip our hat the farthest. As you know, a trophy is to be given, and I believe we can all agree that she is the worthiest recipient. Her special effects made this play what it is. Without her ability to make the ideas reality, we wouldn't have a show at all. And, I must say, fucking yourself to death with knives – a masterpiece."

"Thank you so much," Bonnie said lightly.

"Cheers! Speech! Speech!"

Edward exited the room as Bonnie began to speak, "I am grateful to have gotten the opportunity to go so deep this time," she said. "Each piece was very special to me, and your accolades are humbling. I held my breath each time our protagonist reached a new room, worried that this would be the one that she could see through. It's a bummer that she didn't see it all, but they never do, do they? I specifically want to thank Magdalena for helping me behind the scenes. I couldn't have pulled it off without you."

"You are absolutely welcome!" the whore exclaimed.

Edward returned and sat the trophy on the table in front of Bonnie. By the flickering candlelight, Lucy got a good look, gasping when the shape took form in her mind. A perfectly preserved human head was impaled on a brass stand. The skin was leathery against the skull, the lips receding to reveal perfectly shaped teeth. The eyes appeared plastic, but shined as though they had cried recently.

"Our trophy, as you all remember, is a symbol of what we have accomplished. My father began this enterprise many years ago, and he would haunt me forever if he wasn't allowed to participate in the afterlife. To you father," he said, caressing the head's jaw, "And, to you Bonnie. Well deserved."

The group broke out into applause, the sudden sound cracking through Lucy's ears, rattling her temples.

"It is with humility that I accept this award." Bonnie said, as tears filled her eyes. She wiped them away with the knuckle of an index finger, and composed herself, clearly filled with pride, but unwilling to show it.

Lucy questioned if the trophy was the actual head of Edward's father, or just another prop to shock her. She had a strong sense that it was the real thing, but there was no way to know for sure just by looking, and she wasn't going to ask.

Back in his chair, Edward quieted the applause with a look. He was like a dark prince with minions supplicated. He sat so straight that it looked like his body was floating just above the chair seat, and only the table was preventing him from drifting away.

"Now, as is customary, we open the floor for questions." Edward spoke softly, his eyes moving to look into Lucy's, but his head remaining forward. Lucy sat, unnerved and baffled, until Edward spoke to her directly. "Well, Lucinda, please pay attention. Now is the time for you to speak. Honestly, it isn't a wonder that you have fallen so far."

"Questions?" she asked.

"Yes! Shit! Questions. Ask them," Edward shouted, his cool demeanor cracking.

"Why are you doing this?"

Bonnie laughed and said, "They do always ask that first, don't they?"

"The simple people need their simple answers," said Roger. "You see Lucinda, there is no answer to that question, except for me to counter with, 'Why not?'"

Edward looked amused by the answer, then added his own input. "You have felt boredom, haven't you Lucinda?"

"Yes."

"Exactly, and no one likes boredom. Imagine if that was all you ever felt. In that situation, one can either wilt and submit, or grow and invent. We chose the latter."

More laughter from the peanut gallery.

"So, you like fucking with people. Why don't you just call it what it is, instead of pretending it is some grand design that..." Lucy began to choke and cough, her body heaving. Try as she might, she could not catch her breath, then came movement in her belly, and acid in her throat. A few dry heaves, and she was vomiting her turkey dinner onto the floor. She convulsed and spewed the meat again and again as her hosts laughed hysterically.

Lucy had never been sick for a crowd, and she wasn't enjoying the experience. When it finally felt as if her stomach had nothing more to give up, the cramp in her middle began to release and she sat up and wiped her mouth with the back of her hand. Her head rested on the back of the chair, her body twitched.

Where is death? Why is he so late?

Her vision was thrown askew, and she could no longer get an accurate image of the table. She could hear their snickers, she could feel the psychotic breath that they exhaled, but she could not see them properly. When Edward spoke, she begged her ears to ignore the sounds. She begged her entire body to cease function.

The beating of her stubborn heart mocked her.

"Disgusting little Lucy, can't you see? It *is* a design. This play was designed, and the world is designed. Both by me."

Without lifting her head from the chair, she spat bile onto the table. "You are just an insecure frat boy that happens to own everything. Without the cash, you would have gone from stuffed in a locker, directly into selling vacuum cleaners door-to-door. Now can we get this last supper moving? Kill me already."

"Last supper? No. You will have many more meals, because I and my fellow thespians, are generous. Even the trash has a place, and we will soon show you where that is." Edward raised his glass in the air once again, and the rich sheep followed suit. "I declare that the question portion of the evening is now over. May I assume that we would all like to skip the final pleasantries, and move directly to the end?"

"Absolutely, let's take the trash to her new home," Bonnie blurted.

The sentiment was obviously shared by everyone at the table as they all rose at once. Edward motioned toward the swinging door, and they cackled as they filed through. Lucy had not stood up, and Edward gave her a look, but remained silent. His right hand was still extended, but his left entered a pocket to remove a small black object. He flashed it for her to see. It was a single button, and the mystery of whether her collar was the real deal was finally revealed.

Edward led her through the swinging door, out to the large entryway. The stairs looked so real, yet Lucy wondered if it was all a well-built façade. She expected to be taken to some far-off room that she had yet to see, perhaps down the left hallway above the stairs, but the group had gathered in a semi-circle near the wall directly across from the staircase. It was the place that she would have expected to be the entryway to the house, but featured a simple wall and nothing more.

Or, so she thought.

Edward placed his hand on a section of the wall and pushed. A large rectangular chunk pushed outward into darkness. Bonnie entered first, and as she stepped through, a light turned on to reveal another hallway. The sight instantly angered Lucy. She had been led through so many hallways, so many rooms and doors. When would it all end? How far would this crazy go?

It turned out, that it wouldn't go much further. Just beyond one more door was the end of her road.

A large room, modestly lit. A floor of painted concrete; blue. Walls with no adornment. And cages.

Eight large cages, four on each side of the room. The same that might be found in the bowels of a zoo; dank and dirty, though these cages did not contain the beasts of exotic lands. This was a menagerie of human beings. Defeated people so used to their state of being, that they had no reaction to six free individuals entering their space.

It was without her consent that Lucy's knees dropped from under her, her slack arms causing her hands to smack into the concrete. Several of her knuckles split, and her blood smeared across the azure surface. She peered into the cage nearest to her, where a woman lay on a worn blanket. The skin of the woman was like dark plaster, and her hair matted with the heavy grime of time and neglect.

"Back on your feet. We aren't quite there yet," Henderson chortled, as he grabbed her armpit and yanked her up. As he let her go, she collapsed again, and Edward instructed the fictitious government agent to carry her. Henderson yanked her up again, this time she felt a crack in her shoulder, but that pain would have to be put on hold. Now wasn't the time.

Lucy's head banged against the tall man's back as he walked, causing the cages to shake as they passed. The distorted view of the caged prisoners reminded her of *Planet of the Apes*. It was her father's favorite movie. He had always told her that there was a lesson to be learned in the film, refusing to tell her what it was. As a child, she didn't really get it, but she had a better idea now.

The last two cages were empty, and everyone stopped at the nearest on the left. Inside the cage was a light brown blanket folded up and a dog's water bowl. Roger took a bottle of water that sat on the floor and poured some into the bowl, sloshing it about, and getting the blanket wet. Edward pulled two protein bars from his pocket, smushed from the heat, and tossed them inside as Roger unlocked the padlock holding the cage shut. The lock was immense and opened by a key that Roger stashed in his pocket.

As Roger pulled the bars outward, Lucy's breath rushed from her body. Her face became hot, and her fingertips went numb. Sweat beaded and then dripped from her brow. This was it. The final destination.

From one cage to another. At least this one wasn't colored orange.

Small miracles.

Bonnie took the initiative to push Lucy inside the cage, which she did with immense anger. As Lucy collapsed into her new prison, she looked up into Bonnie's face and saw inscrutable madness. Where had she gotten such hate for Lucy? Was it even for her, or something completely separate? She had the face of a person who simply hated being.

Roger grinned at her and closed the cage, clicking the lock shut as he said, "I'll see you soon. Very soon." He walked back out of the room, with Henderson following closely behind him. When Magdalena the whore noticed that they had left, she scurried to catch them. Edward stayed to look at her for a little longer. As Bonnie was leaving, she stopped and looked back, waiting for her leader.

"It has been, and will continue to be, a pleasure Lucinda," he said. "Get used to your confinement, you will not leave here again. Your world has shrunk even more. It is a cruel truth for you that my existence could be so vast, while yours could be so insignificant." He smiled again, biting his bottom lip lightly. He had once been incredibly sexy to Lucy, then changed into a shadow of beauty. Now, he could only be considered attractive if the Devil himself was a looker.

"Fuck you," she told him.

"Ha! A one note firecracker. I am going to let you recouperate for the rest of the day. My gift to you."

"I don't need your precious gifts."

"Trust me," he said simply, then walked one cage over. Inside lay a woman less filthy than the rest. The girl was young, she looked more alert than the others had. As Edward approached, the girl cowered into her blanket. Lucy didn't think that she could be over sixteen.

Edward rapped his hands against the young girl's cage, and she immediately responded by throwing her blanket off. She got on her hands and knees, and backed herself to the bars of her cage. When she was close, she pulled her pants down and pressed her bare ass to the bars. Lucy could tell that the girl had done this many, many times.

When Edward thrust into her, the girl whimpered slightly, and Lucy's eyes refused to close or look away. She watched as the man gripped the bars and pushed into the girl again. With the third thrust, he grunted and held himself in place for a few seconds. After, he buttoned his pants and walked toward Bonnie, who turned and followed him out of the room.

"I still don't see how you can enter these animals," Bonnie said.

"Maybe you would understand if you had a cock." was Edwards response. Then they were gone. The door closed, and the air fell silent.

Lucy felt as if her heart was going to implode. She moved to one side of the cage, then the other. Again. Then again. She slammed her body into the bars and screamed. She couldn't live this way; trapped in a box. Slamming her head and shoulders into the bars, she hoped to knock herself unconscious, but her mind was a stubborn shit. Blood trickled from several places in her skull, yet still she remained conscious.

An animal that knew her days in the sun were gone.

CHAPTER 5

Fast forward. Just how far forward was a guess not worth making. Weeks. Maybe more. The only thing that mattered now was that it was feeding time.

Edward entered with the black bucket. This was the fourth time that Lucy had been through this, and she was getting the hang of it.

At the first cage, Edward reached into the bucket, grabbed handful of protein bars and tossed them through the iron bars. The woman encaged there frantically snapped them up, desperately reaching for one that had fallen outside the cage. Her fingertips were three inches from the precious bar of food and she screeched her frustration at not being able to add it to her collection. Edward laughed at her but made no move to kick it closer.

He repeated the process at the next cage. The only man in the room lived in this one, and though he was too far away for Lucy to ever get a good look, she knew him to be feeble and mangled. He was unable to move as quickly as the first woman, but luckily, none of his food bounced off the cell bars.

The next two cells got their share, though one of the women screamed a complaint that her portion wasn't large enough. Lucy knew by now that it was the luck of the draw. Whatever Edward grabbed is what you got; any complaint would fall on deaf ears.

As Edward approached her cage, Todd stood beside him; it wasn't the first time that her deceased husband had shown his despicable face. He had been spending quite a bit of time around here lately, often not saying anything, just looking at her with accusatory glares and unbecoming hand gestures. When he did speak, it was nothing but whining. "Why did you let me die?" That kind of thing. It was annoying, but she was getting used to it.

Todd was nipping at Edward's heels, trying to peer over his shoulder and see how much was left for Lucy. At her first feeding, she got twelve bars, but didn't yet know the rules of this part of the game. She ate three or four of them each time she got hungry and they were gone too soon. She did not know that Edward would take so long to return. By the time he did come back, she was gelatin in her cage; starving and weak. That time she had only received seven bars, so she forced herself to ration. Still, she had been without food for what felt like days, but in this place, it could have been hours.

Edward swung the bucket toward her cage and allowed the remainder of the protein bars to rain into her home. Lucy scooped them towards her, as if at any moment they could be taken by an imaginary friend that didn't like to share. Only seven again. Only seven!

But wait, two had bounced onto the floor. Two more precious chunks of life. She slammed her body toward the side of the cage, throwing her arm through the bar and reaching. Her perspective couldn't be trusted, but it seemed like she could get to one if she just stretched a bit further. Just a bit.

As she tried in vain, Edward turned his bucket upside down and placed it over both of the errant bars, then sat down on the top and smiled at her. Lucy snatched her arm back like a reverse snake strike, lest Edward decide to touch her. He had yet to come to her the way he had the young girl. She knew that it was a matter of time, and frankly didn't know why it hadn't happened already.

Todd was still standing next to Edward, and Lucy couldn't help but tell him to go away. Edward assumed the words were directed at him, and answered, "I'm not going to do that just yet."

He had not spoken to her since the moment that she was thrown into the cage, and it was strange to hear his voice. A voice that had become her god; the voice that held her life in its jaws. She had missed it.

"How are you adapting to your new place?"

"I've stayed in better."

"Not much, I would wager," he said, tapping his foot on the floor. It wasn't a constant rhythm, and Lucy got the feeling that he was tapping out a song. Yes, she was sure she had heard it before, but couldn't place it.

Edward reached down and poured some of the water from the jug into her bowl. Luckily the bowl was deep, and she was able to ration enough to stay alive between feedings, though several times she had thought about drinking it all at once. Give it a few days after that and Hell would be a memory for someone else to remember.

Tap. Tap. Tap.

"I am happy to see that your spirits haven't broken yet," Edward said.

"Why? I should think that breaking my spirit is the whole point."

"Sure. It absolutely is, but the watching you reach your breaking point is the sweetest part. I'm happy that I still have more to watch."

Todd sat down next to Edward. He banged his hand against the cage, creating an earth shattering rattle than only she could hear. Lucy flung her hands up to her ears and grimaced. The sudden thunderous noise was too much to handle after such a long stretch of pure silence.

"Stop. Stop. Stop! Fuck Todd, knock it off!"

Edward leaned forward and giggled. He clapped his hands together, and rubbed them slightly, as would a mad scientist with a maniacal plan.

"Oh, goody, goody. I love this part. They are doing their job. My hat is off to my father. A sonofabitch he was, but his ideas are eternal."

Both Lucy and Todd looked up at Edward in confusion. Lucy lowered her hands to say, "What?"

"The hallucinations. It was my father's idea to put the morning glory seeds in the protein bars. I hear that in can be a very introspective trip, but I have never tried it. Drugs are an excuse for the ignorant to forget their ignorance."

"The bars are drugged?" she asked.

"If repeating what I just said will help you understand, by all means, go for it. Yes, they are drugged. Taken in large doses, morning glory seeds are quite the hallucinogen. Another gift to my menagerie."

So, it wasn't the lack of sustenance, exhaustion, or pain. It was her food. The same food that she had no choice but to continue to eat, like someone stranded at sea, killing themselves with saltwater.

Tap. Tap. Tap.

He gave her one more look, then stood to leave. He raised the bucket, then snatched up the protein bars. First, making as if to take them with him, but tossing them onto the cage, allowing the tainted food to rain down on Lucy's head.

"Enjoy those, I must be off. There is a party tonight, and you are the guest of honor. Try and look your best."

Lucy didn't really absorb the information, instead zoning in to the tapping that Edward had made with his foot.

"Hello!" she yelled.

186

Edward turned, "What?"

"Hello. Lionel Richie. You were tapping it with your foot. I wouldn't have taken you for a fan."

"Of course, I am. Have you ever seen the video? Pure evil."

Then he was gone and Lucy was left to wait for the party, whatever that meant. She stared into the package of one of the protein bars, then tore it open. Lifting it up close to her eyes, she tried to find the seeds he referred to. The bar was a conglomerate of things she couldn't discern.

Lucy took a bite and chewed slowly.

Joy filled the air. The entire student body had suddenly shed all their stresses and sense of responsibility was thrown out with last semester's garbage.

The rapping on her door was extremely loud, but one would have to pound to be heard with all the noise out in the hall. Finals were over, and that meant that every guy in the dorm was going to do their best to pass out drunk with their dick inside someone, and every girl was going to feign disinterest until they drunkenly let them.

Lucy ignored the first knock, and the second, attributing the interruption to the countless crazies clamoring in the halls. On the third knock, it seemed like her visitor was trying to break down the door. Todd was getting annoyed with the noise, but not as much as he was when she removed his hand from her panties and put her shirt back on.

She couldn't have expected her father to be on the other side of the door, as well kempt as she remembered, and she was immediately embarrassed by her state of undress.

"Who's the fucking old guy? Just close the door!" Todd bellowed.

"Hi princess," her father said as a large inebriated specimen knocked him in the back. "Can I come in?"

The answer was no, but she made room for him anyway. Todd sat up on her bed, visibly pissed off. He didn't bother to put his shirt back on, or button up his pants, though he did light a cigarette. He knew that she forbade him to smoke in her room, but he was punishing her defiance with tobacco plumes. "What the fuck, Lucy?"

"This is my father. Dad, that's Todd."

Neither exchanged any pleasantries, though both seemed to be sizing up the other. It was her father that spoke first, turning his eyes back to Lucy. It only took four words to send Todd into a frenzy.

"You can do better."

Todd shouted multiple fucks, shits, and bitches. It was babble of the lowest order, and her father didn't flinch. His lack of response angered Todd to the point that Lucy worried he would get physical.

"Babe, just go to the party, I'll find you in a little bit. Okay?"

His fury lowered its guard slightly, and with much protest, he left her dorm room, slamming the door behind him. She heard him shout for a beer, then turned back to her father.

"What are you doing here?" she asked.

"I came to check on you. See how you were. I gotta say, I'm disappointed."

"Well fuck you, dad. How long has it been anyway? A decade? More? How did you find me?"

"I've kept up with you and it has been twelve years. I thought I taught you how to keep time better than that."

Lucy sat down on her bed. She had planned to put on pants, but just didn't care anymore. She would get this man through the door and back out of her life as soon as she could, then she would go out there and find Todd. She would apologize like crazy then bring him back to finally let him have what he had been pushing for over three months.

"Well, you've seen me, so I guess you can go," Lucy said.

Her father averted his eyes, making her realize that she was sitting with her legs open.

"Give me a minute to explain."

"You already did that. I read the note. You couldn't do it anymore. How much more specific could you possibly get. That note was pure poetry," Lucy said, sarcastically.

"I get it. You have an attitude. You're mad. Just suck it up and listen."

She wanted to scream but didn't make a peep.

"I couldn't stay with your mother. We hadn't loved each other for a long time. I am not sure we ever did. I found someone else to be with but I wouldn't leave until I had taught you everything you needed to survive. I couldn't allow myself to leave you unprepared."

"Well, that is mighty magnanimous of you, father. If I say thank you, will you leave?"

"I got you ready for the world, Lucinda. If you apply what I taught you, nobody will ever be able to keep you from success."

"Did you come here to get recognition?"

"Don't I deserve some?"

"No, dad. No, you don't. The fathers that stick around deserve something, but those that take off so they can fuck someone else deserve a heart explosion. I am good at figuring people out. I'm good at standing on my own. I always scan the room as soon as I enter, and I never put my back to the door if I can help it. I know five different ways to kill someone with the shit in my purse, and do you know what all of that got me?"

"Safety," her father said, without hesitation.

"No. It got me nothing but annoyance. Do you think I enjoy constantly looking over my shoulder? How many times do you think that knowing my surroundings has ever saved me in the city?" She put her hand up as her father made to speak. "Save it. The answer is none. Now leave."

"I need you to understand."

Lucy pushed him toward the door.

"I understand fine. You feel justified and I am going to let you." Lucy opened the door and pushed him into the hall. "Now leave. Go and be Thomas Holzer, because you quit being my father twelve years ago. And yeah, I know how long it's been."

She closed the door, then went to find where Todd had thrown her jeans.

Waking up in a cage is about as satisfying as pissing upside down. Speaking of, Lucy had to go. Her new home was not equipped with a toilet and plumbing, so she had to make do with squeezing herself as far through the bars as possible and aiming for a drain in the floor. She couldn't see them all, but she thought there was a drain for each cage.

The ground was sloped slightly, but not enough that it ran all the piss down the drain so she lived in a perpetual stench. As far as shit went, she would take the story of that experience to her grave.

As she was doing her business, Lucy heard a low voice, "You scream in your sleep."

Finishing up quickly, Lucy asked, "Who said that?"

No answer.

"Come on, who said that?"

"I did," came the voice from a cage on the other side of the room.

"You're talking. You never talk. None of you do."

"Yes, we do, but you kind of lose interest after a while. You'll see," the woman said, shifting her body so that Lucy could better see her. "Sit in here long enough, you realize just how little meaning words really have."

"How long have you been in there?" Lucy asked.

"How the fuck am I 'sposed to know? Long time, but not the longest. That honor belongs to those closest to the door. Let's see, eighteen months, plus the rest, but I could only guess on the rest."

"How are you sure about the eighteen months?"

"Simple math. Nine times two."

It took Lucy longer than it should have to understand what the woman was saying, but when she did, her response caught in her throat.

"You've...had babies? Babies in here?"

"We all have, except for that little one next to you. Not sure how she gets so lucky."

He rapes them all. Why hasn't he done it to you?

"My advice," the woman continued, "Just let it happen when it comes. You won't be able to stop it, and after enough times, it sort of becomes the best part of your day."

"How can you say that?!"

"Look, new trash, don't go thinking you can judge me or any of us. What seems like hell to you now is nothing but cupcakes and ice cream. You'll learn that the morals and principles that existed out there won't mean shit to you once you've been in here long enough."

"You seem awfully pissed off at me for someone who hasn't said a word since I got here."

"What about this situation do you think would make me happy? That bucket he brings, full of our precious food – it hasn't changed size. With each new mouth they bring in, that's less for the rest of us."

"That isn't my fault," Lucy cried.

"I know. Don't take it personally, but you took some of my food away, and I'm going to be bitter for a while. Wait 'till they bring in another, and you'll understand."

Sitting back against the bars, as far away from the piss river as possible, Lucy contemplated the woman's words. She couldn't imagine a time when rape wouldn't matter to her, but even more, couldn't believe that the woman who now took pleasure in these assaults. Lucy had believed herself to be at the bottom. Bedrock. Now she knew that time in a cage would be a powerful drill that could take her much further down, to the fire that bellows deep.

"He said something about a party. What did that mean?"

"We all get a welcome party."

"A what?"

"Soon, a bunch of folks who use silver spoons like lollipops will waltz in here with their fancy clothes, eat hors d'oeuvres while they stare at the new specimen in the gallery. You. The newest piece of filth that they can look down on to feel how powerful they are."

"That's horrible!"

"Of course it is but there is a silver lining. Some of them find it amusing to throw food at us. When they do, I hope you learn real quick to toss your pride out of your cell and start eating. They'll laugh, but you can drown out a lot of sound when you chew."

"Have you ever tried to get out of here?"

"Best put all 'o that out your mind. Now leave me be, I want to get a nap in before those rich bastards get here."

The woman rolled over, using her crusted old blanket as a pillow.

"Wait, what is your name?" Lucy asked.

"It's Grace. Now shut the fuck up."

Taking a cue from her new friend, Lucy rolled up her blanket and laid her head down. She was dying to sleep, but that only made her more awake. She didn't want these people to see her at her most vulnerable.

As she rested, she slowly munched on a protein bar and thought of what it might be like to be pregnant and give birth in a place like this.

Where are the children?

It didn't matter. They weren't here and here was all she would ever know.

CHAPTER 6

When Lucy saw Grace wake from her slumber, she attempted further communication, but was ignored. She had so many unanswered questions, but she wasn't sure how she would use the information even if she got the answers. Her stubborn inner voice was still refusing to quit and she had a nagging hope that maybe an opening for escape could be found during whatever this party turned out to be.

Her father had come to pay her a visit and sat in her cage. She resented him for taking up so much of her precious little space, but he wasn't talking to her either. Maybe he had come to keep an eye on her; protect her.

Bullshit. He is here to judge you.

Lucy downed another protein bar in two bites. It would have been much smarter to save the food, but she felt the need to have as much energy as she could for the party. She needed to be alert, not to let any opportunity pass. She realized how odd it was that she had sunk right back into the same state of mind she'd had when she had first been kidnapped, even after all she had seen. Hope was a very powerful motivator if you could find it.

Time ticked, ticked. Lucy grew drowsy once again and thought of eating yet another protein bar when the light began to dim. Lucy rose to her knees and looked through the top of her cage, as if getting her eyes closer to the bars would somehow give her a better view.

All but one line of fluorescent fixtures at the back of the room had been turned off. Near the cages, it was quite dark, and then there was a rumbling sound like the starting of a chainsaw. The sound reverberated so much that it was hard to pinpoint where it was coming from, until finally Lucy saw the circular shadows lowering from the ceiling. She didn't know what was happening until they suddenly clanged on, throwing a perfect beam of light down into her cage; white and blinding. Lucy looked quickly away, as the black spots on her corneas dissipated, she saw that there were beams shining on each cage with an occupant.

Almost as soon as she blinked the shadows from her eyes, the door opened and a whole slew of people filed in. Young men in white tuxedos carried stainless, cloche covered trays. Pretty young girls in revealing spandex bodysuits pushed carts of champagne bottles. They all scurried forward like worker ants, bringing in tables and chairs. Tablecloths and glasses.

Everything was set up in the rear of the room and fluorescent bulbs were turned on to illuminate the area. Each light in the room stayed separate, refusing to play with the others and keeping a wall of shadow in between. A long line of beautifully decorated tables was quickly assembled and covered in elegant accoutrements. The female ants assembled a black curtain toward the side of the room, pushing their carts behind the barrier. The males unsheathed trays of food and began to arrange silver platters with single layers of treats for the rich. Lucy couldn't see from this distance what the food was precisely, but she doubted she would recognize it anyway.

The girls brought forth trays of filled champagne glasses and formed a line leading to the table spread, their spandex suits pushing deep into their ass cracks enough that Lucy was grateful for her filth caked jeans. The men formed a line opposite them with trays of food at the ready. Their tuxedos were expertly pressed; their posture immeasurably stiff. The lot of them stood at perfect attention, creating a road of goodies to follow for anyone lucky enough to attend.

They had to stand that way for a long time. Long enough that Lucy lost interest and turned her back to the bars.

"How long are they going to stand like that?" she asked aloud, not expecting an answer.

"Could be a couple minutes, probably longer. I think he likes to send them in early." Grace answered as she sat up in her cage. Lucy grabbed a protein bar and ripped it open.

"No, new girl, seriously. I told you before, the food will come to you. Don't waste what you have. You are going to be embarrassed as hell, but I promise you are going to eat better than you ever did out there."

Out there. That was what Grace considered the world. How long would it be before she lost track of what it meant to be out there and everything she once knew became the memories of another Lucy, in another time? She wondered how she could get a message out to that Lucy, begging her not to forget about this one.

"You're cracked. Fucked. Dead," said her father.

"Shut up, I'm fine. I'm still here."

"Are you?" he asked.

Who knows?

She sat back and looked over at the help, still lined up like lights on a runway. When the sound of the door opening click-clacked through the room, Lucy saw the collective spandex filled asses tighten. She watched as people flooded the room, dressed in their finest – or not, there was no way for her to know – carrying sparkling handbags, smoking fat cigars, and laughing like their feet were tickled by diamonds.

Against expectations, the party guests did not immediately stop to admire the cages, instead they walked by without even a glance. When the first small group of them made it to the snack line, the lights above turned on, but only in a subtle glow. Just enough for each wealthy individual to compare their wardrobe with each of the others.

As the waiters gave out their final piece of unknown edibles, they rushed away to the sides to get more, and the line moved forward the length of one person. With a new tray filled, they would fill in at the end. It was such a well-oiled machine that Lucy doubted a single guest even noticed. She doubted that half of these people even knew where they had acquired that sparkling glass of champagne, or that rolled up piece of white and green fluff. What was that? Don't eat that. Gross.

Light chatter grew louder as more people filled the room. Edward had not come in yet, but Bonnie had; as well as Henderson. When Roger walked by her cage, he let his fingers brush against each bar. He was the only one that paid attention to her.

After a while of mingling, or schmoozing, or whatever people like this did, the lights dimmed again to announce Edward Wolcroft as he joined the party. The help broke their lines and began to walk through the crowd, offering their wares to anyone willing to look in their direction. Some of the guests touched the waitresses, placing their greedy fingers on places not meant for them, though no disapproval was ever vocalized.

As the champagne made the rounds, sticking like glue to the minds of the crowd, laughter became louder; speech became slurred. Lucy could hear Edward's voice above all the others, but he sounded completely in control. When she caught small glimpses of him weaving through, he never had a glass in his hand. Roger was another story. He seemed to stick to the outskirts of the crowd, downing glass after glass, not waiting for one glass to empty before grabbing another as it passed. He would look in her direction often, smiling at the beginning of the party, but now sneering with contempt.

He hates you. He wants to kill you. What will you do when he decides that now is the time?

"You are taking notes in your mind, just like I taught you. Good girl," her father said, proudly.

"My father is dead, he died when I was twelve, I don't know who you are, but I would thank you to get out of my home."

To Lucy's surprise, he obeyed, now standing near the empty cage across from hers. "You want space? I'll give you space," he said.

"You're a childish asshole. You couldn't possibly be my father."

"You don't know up from down," he said. "Left from right. Dead from alive."

Then he was gone in a blink, just as the crowd hushed at the sound of silverware clinking against glass. Edward required their attention and they were all too happy to give it.

"Thank you all for coming. Most of you have been here before, but I've seen a few new faces here for their first time. This year's play was a complete success and now is the time to view the fruits of our labor."

A loud chuckling forced Edward to stop talking, and as he looked over in her direction, a red-haired woman in a tight green mini-dress choked on her laughter. The man next to her, embarrassed and angry, scolded her with his eyes. She was quiet from then on.

"As I was saying, the main portion of our festivities today is at hand. You all got a glimpse of our masterpieces in the other room, but now you are free to go and investigate them closely. We ask that you please do not touch."

Light clapping came from the audience, and Edward paused to let the soft accolades shower him like drops of pride spit from the gods and monsters above.

"As far as the main attraction," he said, "You have no doubt been dying to see her." The light above Lucy's cage suddenly brightened to the point of blistering. She held her hand to her eyes like a salute as another round of clapping erupted, more uproarious this time. Her father clapped along with the rest. "Her name is Lucinda Holzer, and she is this year's lucky winner. Feel free to examine her at your leisure, but now I bet you want to hear the tale. Am I correct?"

Cheers all around. Thunderous and triumphant. Her father went to stand with the crowd, and she noticed that Todd was there too, though she hadn't seen him come in. Edward began to recount the entire story of her time in his company.

From the moment he met her, he knew that she was the one they had been looking for. He saved her, and then took her. He told of how he convinced her that he was in love with his own mother, laughing as he did so.

"I could almost see the mouse wheel turning in her pedestrian brain!" Edward exclaimed.

He told of the introduction of Roger, and how they meticulously placed every prop. He spoke of his genius during their first dinner and the tricks that led to the moment Roger had raped her. He gave the order in which Lucy had traversed the fabricated rooms, and her reactions to each one. Edward did not exaggerate. His words were undiluted truth, and she couldn't stand listening anymore.

Her hands against her ears, Lucy began to hum to herself.

Hello. Is it me you're looking for?

She hated the song.

Hated it.

She could see them laughing along to his animated retelling. Lucy had often felt like a joke in her life, but she never knew that she was such a funny one.

Where are you now, Lucy? Where are you when I need your help? What am I supposed to do? Answer me!

Do it! You live. Right here in this cage, you live. If that doesn't suit you, then you choose door number two. There isn't a third choice, and frankly, I don't care what you pick.

It was a lengthy story time, and when Edward finished, Lucy's nails had made dents in the flesh around her ears. As she moved her hands back, they stuck like plungers attempting to unclog her brain. Her own internal voice had turned its back on her for now, her father and ex had vanished, so she was stuck with only herself as a mob of people shambled like overly respectable zombies in her direction.

Some passed right by and continued out of the room. Others stopped to see the previous years' models in their cages, but the majority crowded around her light bubble, pointing, jeering, and laughing.

As Grace had promised, small bits of food were tossed into her cage, sometimes hitting her, sometimes bouncing across the floor of the cage leaving colorful trails like a painted rock skipped on ice. Lucy looked at all the food, feeling paralyzed. It was only when the crowd rumbled its displeasure that she realized that they wanted to watch her feast on their offerings.

She ate; each bite a flavor her tongue had never encountered. With each taste, her show drew applause. She was a penny fountain granting wishes of shame. There seemed to be no end to the amount of pleasure that the crowd derived from her eating their leftovers, and her embarrassment began to shift into a sort of sick pride against her will. Lucy wondered if this was why the carnival geeks of old were willing to lower themselves to such a spectacle. They ate blood and guts, not caviar or colorful plumes of delicious mush, but still, she thought the level of enjoyment must have been similar.

Lucy looked over in the direction of Grace's cage but had to shift her body to see between the legs of her admirers. Grace didn't have the crowd that she had, but there were still plenty to rain down her dinner. The woman looked happy; thrilled. This was the highlight of the year. Christmas in a cage.

Her own cup was overflowing, and Lucy began to feel guilty. She could see now, more than ever, why Grace would resent her. She was an invader. The flavor of the month.

She was Tutti-Frutti.

Someone in the crowd said, "She's covered in filth!"

Another said, "No different than she looked before. Trash is trash."

And, "The cage looks good on her, but that smell! Can you believe it?"

Tears started forming as the weird pride she had felt as the center of attention flew away on the winds of realization. Still, she scooped up a splatter of black caviar with her index finger and licked it like icing on a cake. Todd was kneeling by the side of her cage now, trying to console her. His demeanor was something she never remembered from him. He was gentle; concerned.

He isn't real.

None of this is real at all. These people aren't here. This food is a figment of your fucked mind. Any moment you will wake and the only reality will be steel bars and time. Plenty of time to wonder if there was ever anything you could have done or if you truly were doomed from the start. A woman with a father that couldn't teach enough; a wife that never learned the simplest of lessons.

When she looked around and found that the crowd was gone, it wasn't a surprise. Time was playing its evil tricks. Could she even be sure that there ever was a party at all if not for the sweet taste in her mouth? Even that could be a lie.

Morning Glory seeds he said. Did she dare believe any of it? Maybe her father was right, and she was only a corpse, gurgling last thoughts beneath a thick layer of sod and drying roses.

But no, there were still people. There was still a decimated hors d'oeuvres table, a fraction of its former glory. There was still enough spandex to stretch across the world, shoved into the smallest, perkiest creases. The clean-up had begun, and the guests were moving on. Only a few stragglers remained, but all the time that they had allotted for Lucy had passed, and before she could blink three times, they were gone. The waitresses were gone. The waiters in their adorable monkey suits gone. She was alone again. The event of the year passing without even a goodbye kiss.

"What did I tell you?" Grace said, shockingly satisfied.

"You said it. I ate."

"Don't seem so down. This was the best day that you are going to have for a very long time. The sooner you settle in and get used to the little things, well, you'll be happier."

"I'll be happy with tainted food, rape, and boredom?"

"Yes. You will. I was where you are now, and I wouldn't have believed it then either. But the mind and body are resilient. They adjust. If they don't, you die. Either way."

Lucy didn't care about what might come later, only what was now. Now she had a full belly and an empty heart. She needed to sleep and forget. She needed to dream of something better than this. As long as she was able to dream of better times, then she would never lose them completely.

You sound like a fucking greeting card.

Todd approached her in the dark, stinking of gin and pussy. There was streaks of red running the length of the sky, and she was lying in leaves. As he got closer, her world shook, making her bones rattle in their skin. He was upon her when she woke.

Lucy's cage was rocking erratically. It took a long moment for her to remember where she was. She had been under the sky, now she was under an obtrusive bright light. The food she had piled for later was jiggling across the floor of her cage, dancing like jumping beans.

It was Roger that was disturbing her. Roger who had both his hands wrapped tightly around the bars, shaking his entire body in unabashed anger. When he saw that she had come to, he slowed his spasms, eventually calming completely and kneeling down to her. His expression was similar to the one she had seen it morph into as he drank at the party, he was still wearing the same clothes he wore then. A navy-blue suit, off-white shirt, and bright purple tie. How long had the party been over?

He still had a drink in his hand, though it was beer this time. Coors light – the same beer her husband used to drink. She had imagined that Roger would only drink the finest, most expensive ales, so the *silver bullet* seemed a smidge out of place in his trembling paw.

He laughed at her.

"It's time, bitch."

"Time?"

"Don't play dumb," he said, taking a sloppy swig.

"I live in a cage, and I have a hard time keeping up with current events, so no – I don't know what you mean."

It was still surprising to Lucy how she could still hold on to her sarcasm. Even without understanding the passing moments of time, she was still able to spit derision like watermelon seeds. It made her happy knowing that at least a tiny part of her still resided in her mind, in some far-off room, furnished with a blow-up bed and black-out curtains.

After downing the rest of the swill in the bottle, Roger said, "It's time to finish what I started a month ago. It's time for you get to get what's coming. Disgusting urchin. I'm gonna fuck you 'till you scream; happy or sad."

It wasn't the impending rape that surprised Lucy, it was that she had been in a cage for a month that caught her attention. She couldn't figure out if she was shocked at being in there for so long, or appalled that it had only been such a short length of time. What sometimes seemed like weeks, often only felt like minutes.

That was when the notion of rape took hold.

"No Roger, you can't do this!"

"Stop calling me Roger! Roger is dead. You saw the corpse smeared out there," he said, throwing his arm toward the direction of the door. He was beyond drunk, Lucy realized. "Now, I know you've seen the other trash do it, so follow...just do...just come here. Drop your filthy fucking pants and press your ass against the bars so I can get a good look."

He was already undoing the clasp on his slacks, having a lot of trouble with the process. His body swayed, and he cussed at his inability to unfasten a simple pair of pants. He pulled on them hard when finesse didn't work. Eventually, there was a slight tearing sound, and the blue slacks fell to the floor. His underwear were not those normally worn by males, instead satiny black. Roger wore women's underwear and Lucy couldn't help but giggle.

At the sound, Roger slammed his hands against the cage. "Keep laughing! You'll stop soon enough. Now get your fucking trash ass over here."

He pulled the panties down to the floor, and Lucy jumped into action without knowing what she was doing. Her hand simply flew out in front of her and she watched it in slow motion. Roger's purple tie was hanging low as he bent to pull the pants and underwear from his legs. Lucy's hand deftly grabbed the cravat and pulled.

Roger's head slammed into the cage bars, his nose and mouth pressed between two of them; spit and snot dripping onto the cage floor. Before he could compose himself, Lucy reached the hand holding the necktie out of the bars and spun the silk around Roger's neck.

Once.

Then, twice.

He tried to push himself away, turning his head. She pulled back again, even harder this time. There wasn't as much tie to hold on to, but she wouldn't let go. She could see herself now, from the corner of her brain. She watched herself and saw the determination. Even with very little energy left in the recesses of her flesh, she would never let go.

She yanked back with stubborn force, causing Roger's skull to grind into the bars. His feet were slipping against the concrete floor as he tried to stand, but Lucy held him in place. Roger's arms flailed as he tried to reach behind him; to release himself from her clutches. He only managed to bang his knuckles against the bars.

Lucy arched her back and put her feet up to a bar apiece. Pushing back with the strength of her legs, she was able to fully cut off the air to Roger's brain. She couldn't see his face, but she could see the rims of his ears redden quickly. She held fast; he struggled.

Todd was beside her then, accusing her of murder. The second of her life, he said repeatedly. She ignored him and pulled tighter. Roger was all flying limbs and death gurgles, but he wasn't dying. It was taking longer than she thought, but his body did begin to slacken, and as he put up less and less of a fight, she pulled even tighter still. A pool of piss spread across the floor below him and that may have been the most satisfying part about killing Roger. The man who had treated his own wife like shit, had been forced into penetrating her against his will, who had died and risen again; a strange sort of Christ. The man that became all new and was now dying for his transformation.

He was never those things.

He was all those things.

He was dead.

Lucy let go of the tie only after several more minutes of force. She wanted to crush his throat if she could. She didn't want to take the chance of him coming back to life with his voice intact. She couldn't handle anymore lies from the dead.

When she did let go, his heavy body slipped down to the floor and splashed in his own urine. She could hear Grace clapping for her. Even the young girl in the next cage was cheering her on, but her body quit. Lucy sank down low into the cage floor like pancake batter mixed with too much buttermilk.

She knew that she must rise. She had to check the body for the key to the lock that held her prisoner. She knew that he must have it on him, but it would have to wait.

Sleep would not be denied.

Lucy didn't wake again on her own. She was helped into consciousness by the constant shouts of Grace and the others. None of them felt this was any time to take a nap, and while that seemed like perfectly sound logic, her body and mind were still operating on the absurd.

When she was finally sitting upright, Grace shouted at her "Thank Christ! Now check him. He has keys. That fucker always has keys!"

It took Lucy a moment to understand why she would want any keys. What would a key get her? There was nothing out there for her, she thought. She had seen what out there had to offer, and it was much safer in the cage.

Snap out of it! You've been looking for your chance. At least, whenever you are in your right, sane mind. This is it! That moment that you have looked for. You created it by killing that rapist shit laying outside. Now check his pockets for the keys. Save yourself. Save them.

"Move new girl! Someone will come back in here soon. Get the keys," Grace said, politely, yet stern, like a nun teaching geometry to a small heathen child.

Lucy did finally reach out of the cage, but before she was able to check any pockets, she caught a glimpse of Roger's pale purple face. His tongue was sticking out slightly, and the tip was a dark purple color. His head had fallen at a weird angle, making it look broken. Somehow, his eyes still looked lecherous, and before she looked for the key to her escape, she used two fingers to close them. She wouldn't allow him to look at her again.

Then, she spat on him. Those that are above can spit on those below, it is much harder in the reverse. The key was in his front right pocket; the first Lucy checked, though she checked the others just to make sure and found them empty. It was a small, tarnished gold key connected to heavy key chain in the shape of the Statue of Liberty. Instead of holding the torch proudly to the sky, she was smoking a joint and giving a thumbs up.

The key slid into the lock willingly, as if to say, "See, that wasn't so hard." Lucy had to push the cage door open with both of her feet to move the body propped against it. When there was enough room, she pushed her head through, and then her right leg. As soon as she tried to stand, her body collapsed like pick-up sticks. She used the cage to pull herself back up, embarrassed by how she must look. Grace just egged her on. The young girl in the next cage was screaming, and Lucy couldn't tell if it was in ecstasy or fright.

She sat her butt on top of the cage and stretched her legs, slapping them in an effort to restore blood to their unused muscles.

"Okay, now get over here at let me out," Grace said.

It won't work.

"Just a minute," said Lucy as she rubbed her feet. There had been only one key, and unless Edward and his cronies had made a major lapse in judgment, the same key wasn't going to unlock all of the cages. Roger had only brought this one with him because he wanted get his hands on her.

Most of the water in her bowl was gone, but Lucy leaned down and drank the rest once she felt the circulation return to her lower extremities. She also downed the last two protein bars. In doing so, she realized that had she not escaped tonight, she would have had many hungry days ahead of her. Even in a world with limited food, she was still a stress eater.

She walked with unsure footsteps to approach Grace's cage. The woman had the brightest smile that a caged animal had ever sported. It was a smile that Lucy knew was about to be wiped, maybe forever. Reaching out to grab the lock, she squeezed the key tightly, until she could feel her flesh crack open. Lucy reached forward and attempted to unlock her new friend, but the key wouldn't even go in the lock.

As Lucy lowered her hands, she let the key slide from her blood greased palm and tinkle against the concrete.

"What are you doing?" Grace asked.

"There was only one key."

"No..."

"I'm so sorry."

"No."

With tears, Lucy repeated herself, "So sorry."

"FUCK!" Grace screamed. "Fuck, fuck, fuck."

Lucy stood dumbfounded, her face a rising tide of salt water and snot. Grace slammed her hands against her own bars and Lucy watched. She had no other words.

When the woman had calmed herself, she looked back at Lucy and asked, "What are you doing? Go."

"I..."

"No, just go. I don't know what's on the other side of that door, but you go see, and you get the hell out of here. Quit standing there like an idiot."

Lucy did her best to choke back her emotion, trying to become as hard as the bars that held Grace at bay. She reached into the cage and held her hand out to the woman, the only thing she could come up with to show her pain.

The woman didn't take her hand. "No. Don't do that. You don't know me, and I don't want your sympathy. Just go." Then the woman rolled over, using her back as a barrier to what might have been if luck existed in this place.

Lucy took two steps back, then turned herself toward the door. It was time to go.

The young one yelled, "Hey wait! What is happening?"

Lucy didn't look her way, she didn't want to see the crushed hopes of another person. As she got closer to the door, the next set of cages held eyes fixed on her. The next set barely gave her a glance, and the last two didn't seem to have noticed anything at all. They had all already died long ago. Somehow, a small chunk of Lucy was still ticking. A tiny morsel of fleshy acceptance that death wasn't quite here yet. That piece was moving forward, gripping the doorknob that led to "out there". Soon, she would feel the air of the real world again, or that was her hope.

She almost looked back at the cages. She wanted to see her own cage one more time. She wanted to remember what this life was like, even for such a small amount of time, but Lucy didn't look back, and the door creaked as she opened it toward her. The hallway she had come through a month ago was pitch dark.

Dark was normal. Dark was what awaited everyone out there.

CHAPTER 7

When the door closed behind her, Lucy started to feel cold and realized that she hadn't felt the sensation since she had been put in the cage. The orange room had been a human refrigerator, but the cage was a metal desert. Even though she knew the dark hallway to be straight, she still managed to run her tired body into the wall several times, bruising her shoulder.

When at last she came to the end of the hall and placed her hand on the doorknob, Lucy hesitated. It seemed that she always lost her nerve the moment her hand was on the door.

Just go. You've seen the other side.

She had seen the room beyond before, but when she pushed the door open, Lucy found that it was not as she had left it. Where once stood elaborate stairs and arches were now piles of dead house carcass. The stairs were gone, but the bones of what they once were lay in piles around the large room. The expensive floor, which she had never really paid attention to before, had been taken up, and was now just old concrete. Chunks of glue and leftover tile were scattered here and there. Rolls of red carpet that once accented the stairs, now sagged in rolls against a far wall. The arches themselves had been pushed on to their sides and discarded as easily as a toddler's block tower.

The rear, where there was once a long hallway leading to Edward's bedroom, was now virtually empty, with no sign of any of the paintings or other furnishings. There were no doors leading to unknown rooms; no beds marked with blood and shame. Just a massive open room with ceilings far higher than they had been previously. The entire home had been taken apart, piece by piece, and discarded. Lucy had no way of knowing where everything else had gone, but she somehow felt like a piece of herself had been stripped away. She had been held prisoner in a world that wasn't even real. Even as a captive, there was a level of dignity that came with knowing the situation for what it was, but that was now being taken from her too. Lucy felt like her feet were no longer on the ground, instead floating above a pack of lies and silly putty.

In front of all the prop stacks and discarded heaps of building materials, was each of the cadavers she had come across in her travels through the false maze that had been created for her. The pile of Roger's flesh sat against the concrete, his face draped over the bloody chunks. Just next to Roger was Agent Henderson, sitting in his spiked chair, the word of his intestine still repeating itself near Roger's parts.

"'Mother.' You need to get a new line, Henderson," Lucy said, to no one.

Bonnie lay spread eagle as she once had, though her arms weren't bound anymore and the machine wasn't moving. The pile of her mutilated womanhood was arranged on the table, now looking decidedly more fake than it had the first time Lucy had seen it. This was the false corpse that angered her the most. She had felt for Bonnie. *Really* felt for her. The indignity of her death, Bonnie's death, had been the most incomprehensible and hideous in a series of inconceivable situations. Lucy had felt pain when she had seen the woman torn apart by that dildo of death, but now she only wished it had been real. She wanted to see Bonnie suffer what Lucy had already believed her to have done. If it were a possibility, Lucy might flip the switch on the machine herself.

You wouldn't. You don't have it in you.

How the fuck do you know? You tell me over and over to keep going, don't quit. Now look at you! Hanging in the wings, waiting to see what might happen.

At least I'm not angry at a piece of plastic laying on a table.

Fuck you!

She was furious with no outlet. What could she do now? Her mind had the whole of it. This Bonnie was a hunk of plastic and nothing more.

"How do you know? Did you check?" her father said, walking past Lucy. He stood at the end of the table, staring into the gore between Bonnie's legs. "Did you?"

"I don't have to check. I know that Bonnie is out there somewhere, living her charmed life. That is just a special effect that she built to screw with me."

"Maybe," he said. "Maybe." Then, he reached across the table into a pile of Bonnie and grabbed a handful. Her father let the pieces shift in his palm, then squeezed. The pink goop squished from between his fingers, dropping like dead worms to the floor. "Feels real to me," he said.

Lucy walked closer to Bonnie and her father. She took a good long look at what fell from his hands and had to agree. She wasn't sure exactly how a mutilated womb may look, but it seemed reasonable that it would be just like this.

"No. Stop trying to confuse me," she said. "You aren't even real either. A fake person has no place to comment on what else is fake."

"I'm just as real as that woman's fucked up pussy," he said. "Pardon my language, but it had to be said. I am just a manifestation of what was already inside your mind. Those silly flower seeds didn't make me. You did."

From behind her, another voice chimed in. "Me too. I'm here for you. Because of you. Just like him. Just like that poor schmuck sitting in that nail chair." As Todd made the reference, he giggled and went to sit in Henderson's lap. He leaned back and gave the dead man a kiss on the cheek, then grabbed the intestine from between his legs and pretended it was his own cock. Todd swung the thing around and around with a look on his face like an eight-year-old that just made the best joke of his life.

Lucy didn't know which of the men from her former life she was more embarrassed of. Her ex-husband with the mental capacity of a preteen or her father that just nonchalantly dropped the p-word like it was an everyday thing to say to your daughter. Worse, she was getting angrier. The cool air she had felt in the hall was completely gone; now replaced by a warm, clamminess on her whole body. She could feel her blood pressure rise inside and her heartbeats throbbed like bee stings.

All at once, Lucy screamed at Todd and her father, causing their bodies to turn to smoke and drift away as she reached for Bonnie's right arm. She grabbed the rubber wrist of the forged corpse and yanked hard. The flesh tore at the shoulder and pulled away so easily that Lucy fell back on her ass, sliding two feet back across the concrete. Bonnie's bones were nothing but cardboard tubes; her sinew cotton balls and cellophane.

A scream reverberated against the walls, bouncing to and fro until the sound finally settled in Lucy's ears, the familiarity of the voice confirming the sound was coming from her own mouth. Standing back up, she brandished the arm like a cavewoman with a club, beating at Bonnie's face. Chunks of the arm flew through the air in all directions, but Lucy didn't stop until the limb she still held was the size of a small rib-eye steak. Just a wrist, half a palm, and three articulated fingers.

Bonnie's face was unchanged, still in a perpetual state of dead shock.

Lucy dropped the remainder of the arm to the floor, then walked to where she knew the dining room had once belonged. The dining table was gone, as were the plants and candles; real or fake. Boxes were stacked haphazardly to the side of the room, some taped neatly shut, while others still sat opened and half filled with set pieces and junk.

She didn't linger here long, moving quickly through the way she had been led from Edward's office. Her destination was the elevators that hadn't worked before. Lucy could see no reason they wouldn't be running now that she had been caged and effectively erased. With luck, she would ride the metal box to the ground floor and walk right out into the sunshine; half dead, but free. She would find the police and send them to save Grace and the others. Lucy would be a hero.

Her inner voice sighed.

Why? Do you enjoy tormenting yourself? Tormenting me? Why do you persist in thinking that something is going to go the way that you desire it to? Go back to your cage. It's safe there. Ahead of you, there will only be pain.

"I don't know what happened to you," Lucy said aloud. "Keep moving forward, right? That's what we do."

She wasn't listening to herself, but it didn't matter now. Her feet were programmed, and they wouldn't stop until they touched the outside world, or death halted their steps forever.

In the reception room, where Bonnie's desk still sat proudly, she got her chill back. The room was mostly empty now, yet she felt a heavy weight in the air. If there were ghosts in this life, they were here; laughing and joking at Lucy's expense. She couldn't see them, but she felt the pressure they placed on her shoulders. The reception desk didn't have a phone, stapler, or tape dispenser. There was no inbox, outbox, or computer. There was however, a small pad of paper and a pencil sharpened to its last inch.

As she inspected the paper, she found heavy indentations pressed into the pulp. Taking the pencil, she lightly colored the top sheet as she had seen in countless movies. Six words appeared in the negative space within the graphite.

She couldn't begin to fathom the context for the words, or even who wrote them. Perhaps Bonnie was just waxing lyrical about how to end her day. Maybe Edward was musing on what his next grand design would be.

Maybe you wrote it yourself. Maybe you are still trapped in your head in the cage. Hell, maybe you never left home at all. How can you be sure that Bonnie ever existed?

Choosing to ignore her mind, Lucy walked on. The voice inside herself was tainted now. The ability to reason replaced by paranoia and negativity. If anyone was going to see Lucy through to the end, it wasn't going to be that woman in her mind. It wasn't going to be her father, who only seemed to show up to receive credit for what normal fathers did without question. Todd was certainly never going to help, in fact, he probably would do anything to watch Lucy squirm in psychotic hell.

No, Lucy only had this instinctive part of herself now, and she had no way of knowing how long she would have even that much left. Her skin was covered in goosebumps and sweat, her epidermis confused about the state of things. A relatable concept, for sure.

Her eyes trailed to her side, seeing the half-opened door leading back to Edward's office. On the floor, a pool of water stretched out, reflective, like liquid mercury. Without a thought, Lucy mushed the door open. She should move forward to find her way out of this madhouse, but curiosity was another aspect that seemed out of her control.

Inside the room, most of the furniture was gone. The orange room that once held her captive behind a pane of glass had been similarly cleared. The glass was gone. The barrier between her and the world that had seemed so permanent was gone. Edward simply took it away. The red curtain that had acted like eyelids to her prison now sat in a heap on the floor.

It was the smell that took her attention away from her old home behind the missing glass. She had noticed it when she first entered, but now it had grown far stronger as her nose nestled into its rancid perfume.

On her left, the shark tank had been shattered. Most of the water was gone except for the pools on the floor. Coral stood crusty on the floor of the tank and dried plants did death curls, almost wasted away.

It was so lifeless. The never-ending circling of sharks seemed so predictable, like it would go on forever, until Lucy saw the tank as it was now. She longed to watch the path of those sharks once more but all she could see or smell was their necrotizing corpses laying on the wet, cold floor. Edward had not bothered to dispose of his pets, choosing instead to pump out the water and leave them to suffocate on air.

The animals' skin, that once looked so artificial as it split the water, now wrinkled and collapsed in on itself, splitting open in multiple places so that the smell of its extinction filled the air. The stench was not so overwhelming that it was unbearable, leading Lucy to assume that the carnage had occurred long enough ago for it to have dissipated somewhat.

She had given so much meaning to the creatures. They were captive as she was captive. Edward had enslaved them all for his amusement. Now they lay dead and she continued to walk around, experiencing a far different kind of death. She longed for the permanent release that the sharks were enjoying. She wanted her own skin to wrinkle and crack. Her own smell to offend any who came across her.

Instead, she backed out of the room and closed the door, passed Bonnie's desk, and moved on.

The next room held the singular elevator with nothing but an up arrow. Not what she needed at all, but just a few steps beyond it was the door that would lead to the main hall. A few more feet beyond that and Lucy would be pressing the button to call the elevator that would take her down. The end was close enough that the panic set in like a tornado circling her heart, stealing beats, and tossing them aside like fence posts.

The door is locked.

"God, shut up!" Lucy screamed.

But, the knob didn't turn. Not left, nor right. It didn't matter how much force she applied, the knob stayed put. Her body collapsed to the floor and she began to cry. How often now had her survival depended on the opening of a door? Todd sat down next to her and lit a cigarette. He held one out to her, but she waved it off.

"You have to admit," he said, taking a small puff and immediately exhaling like a sophomore in high school out by the railroad tracks just trying to fit in. "This really was predictable."

"You're probably right. Are you going to tell me I should have stayed in the cage too?"

"Not on your life. I was curious to see how far you could get. Besides, the cage is boring. Anyone can see that."

"It's safe though."

"I think that you may have gotten your relativity skewed. Safe is out there. Nothing in here is safe."

"Out there wasn't safe either. I was out there when I got kidnapped, remember?"

Todd took another baby, pansy drag.

"Fine. Then nowhere is safe. Just sit here until they find you, what does it matter?"

Lucy thought about taking her ex up on his cigarette offer, if only to show him how to take a proper drag. "There is another way. I go back through the house. Through the kitchen. Same hallway, same elevators. Just take a few extra steps is all."

"Then why are you still sitting?"

"Because," she said, pretending to think, but knowing full well why she hadn't stood back up. A few moments thought, and she decided to be honest with Todd. "Because, if that way is blocked too, then there really isn't anything. That's the last hope, and I don't want to face it. As long as I sit here, I'm not trapped. Here, I am as free as I can be."

Deciding that a cigarette would really hit the spot, she turned to take the one from Todd's inept hand, but he had gone, leaving only the rancid Marlboro smell in the air as a reminder for her that the conversation really took place. Just like in her past life, Todd was never there when she needed him; only when it suited his own interests.

Despite her fears, Lucy got back to her feet. She hadn't made the decision to stand and she was getting really tired of her body choosing to listen to anyone but her. There was nothing for it now but to move forward. It might take her some time to get to the other side of the house, as distractions were popping up all over.

After only two steps, a loud ding filled the room. The arrow on the elevator button was shining orange, and the metallic noise rattled behind the wall. There was a thunk, and the doors slid open. Edward was looking down at his feet, but when he took the first step off the elevator, he looked up and locked eyes with Lucy once more.

"Well, well. I didn't know it was trash day."

CHAPTER 8

Two thoughts ran through Lucy's head simultaneously, occasionally crashing into each other like bumper cars. The first was too self-defeating to be considered valuable, but she thought it anyway. *Why is it that every single time I decide to keep going with this shit show, I am immediately derailed?* The second thought was, "How do I kill this man right now?"

It was purely by accident that she spoke her second thought aloud, and Edward laughed at her.

"Kill me? Have you still not caught on to what is happening yet? There is no way for you to kill me. You don't win. I win. Me."

"Sometimes the underdog wins," was her response.

"Sure. In sports owned by people like me. People who like a little manufactured drama from time to time. You aren't an underdog, poor little dirty Lucy, because we aren't playing the same game."

"What now? You take me back to my cage, kill me? What?"

Edward backed a few steps and leaned against the wall, inspecting his fingernails. He had his feet crossed, totally relaxed.

"How did you get out anyway?" he asked.

"Your friend Roger is dead again."

"My friend! That's funny. You wouldn't know, but he has been a pain in the ass my entire life. Rich, but not as rich as me.

Powerful, but not as powerful as me. Those types of people just latch themselves on to people like myself. Barnacles impossible to scrape off. You did me a favor."

"Well I guess you can owe me."

Edward laughed for a lot longer than seemed necessary. Enough to double over and literally slap his knee. Lucy had never seen someone do that in real life.

"Lucinda, you are adorable for such a worthless mammal. I've never had so much fun with any of our trash bags before. All they tend to do is scream and cry. Sometimes it's like pulling teeth just to get them to move their slob bodies into the next room. If there is one thing *most* lacking in your kind, it is self-preservation," Edward said, uncrossing his feet and pacing a few steps back and forth. "You've been nothing but a surprise to me. Always fighting. Always willing to find out what's on the other side. You made this year's play very special for us."

"Fuck you," she said as the strength in her legs began to fade again.

He laughed again.

"And then, sometimes you are quite predictable and it reminds me just what you are."

Lucy was tiring and she had to beg herself to stay on her feet. Edward was blocking the door leading back to the dismantled dining room. There was no way that was a coincidence. If he was going to bar her way, and she couldn't get through the locked door on her side, the elevator was the only option. She glanced over at the metal doors and gulped hot air.

"Yeah, now you get it," Edward cackled. "There is only one path, and there only ever was. Every choice you have made was handed to you by me. I own your free will. Now take the elevator. See what you see. Consider it your last vacation."

Looking back to the elevator, she saw her father and Todd waiting there. Their backs were to her, and her father held a newspaper, reading silently. Todd stood like he had bugs in his pants, just like he always did when he had to wait. They were waiting for her, unwilling to miss the next episode. Edward was smiling, still picking small bits of something from his nails; a man without care.

What do you do when your only option is created by someone that means you harm?

Lucy walked to the elevator and pressed the button and the doors parted immediately. Todd entered first, then her father, never looking up from his paper. She couldn't ever remember her father reading a newspaper before. She took the step into the elevator herself, and as she turned, Edward was waving at her.

"You explore, I'll meet you in a bit,"

She noticed that his nails were covered in flakes of dark red as the elevator doors shut.

The elevator was silent as it ascended. Todd knocked on the metal walls, and Lucy was surprised at the hollow sound he made. Her father finished up whatever article he was reading, then tossed the paper down.

"There isn't a damned thing worth reading about anymore," he said.

There were no numbers counting their ascent, nor any sound indicating that they had passed a floor. The only button was a down arrow and she had not needed to press anything to go up. Lucy had never been in an elevator that moved so quietly, so when the doors opened, letting the bright sun wash over her, it was a shock. She closed her eyes to shield them from the blinding glare before letting them slowly crack back open. The heat of the sun felt foreign on her skin. There was a breeze.

A fucking breeze.

She had already forgotten about trivial things like wind, and she wondered how Grace would have reacted, or the poor people in the first cages. She let the warm breeze lick her, the tingling making her arm hair stick up. She looked down to watch the hairs sway and saw just how dirty she had become. The sun had shown her for trash.

The woman tied to the folding chair went unnoticed by Lucy for some time. Lucy didn't see her slack jaw, slit throat, or the bruises that speckled her chest. The sun was too bright and hypnotizing for Lucy to see the blood that dripped from the woman's chin, fingers, and eyes.

Pay attention!

When she spied the corpse, all she could think was - another one. Lucy must have ruined some of the big show by never making it up to the roof. She walked over to the woman, the sun now completely enveloping her. Bonnie had done a good job on the woman. Lucy hated her, but there was no denying the talent. Todd was already at the body, inspecting the woman. He bent his knees and ran a finger through the red puddle under the chair and her father did the same.

The puddle was much redder than the dark stickiness of the other props. Todd looked back at her. Her father stood and smelled his fingers.

Was she...?

"I don't think..." said her father.

She isn't fake.

"This one is real," Todd said.

Everyone agreed at once that they weren't staring at a piece of plastic, but a dead sack of flesh. Looking closer, Lucy realized that she recognized the woman from the party. The same that had interrupted Edward with her drunken outburst.

No! Come on, it is just another dummy. Get up there and look closely. You'll see.

When Lucy picked up the wrist of the woman, there was no doubt. There never should have been. She should never have found herself in a life that would cause her to doubt a dead body's authenticity. This wasn't living. She had just wanted a date with a good-looking guy; to get out of that fucking popcorn shop. Maybe put out and wait a bit while he never called again. There was a time in Lucy's life when that would have been devastating, but now she was holding the wrist of a dead woman. There were no tremors in Lucy's hands now. No tears in her eyes.

There would be soon.

Very soon.

Dropping the dead woman's arm, Lucy turned away from the body and took a few more steps out into the open area of the roof.

Across from her was a mound of old boxes and trash. The rubbish appeared old enough that she doubted if anyone ever bothered with cleaning up there. Near one of the boxes she saw something she wished she hadn't and her eyes closed tight. A skull. A very small human skull.

She rushed over, tripping along the way; skinning her palms, yet barely noticing the pain. The infant's skeleton was contorted so that the eye sockets looked upside down at Lucy She could have fit the rib cage in her bloody palm. The bones had been trampled, leaving shards of what used to be a baby's life.

Lucy waved a fly away from her cheek. The insect flew right back, but she didn't bother with it again. She wanted to look away but somehow knew that what she was seeing was the beginning of the end. There were three more babies in various states of decay piled behind the box, all about the same size. Newborn.

Her father stood far away, but Todd was trying to get a good look at the skeletons.

"Get back!" she screamed at her ex-husband. The idea of someone like him touching the poor children to much for her to handle.

"Are you telling me to leave my own roof?"

Lucy spun around so fast that her vision couldn't keep up, and again she collapsed to the ground. Edward was standing next to the dead woman, his hand resting on her cold shoulder. Todd acted as if he would walk up and hit him, but Lucy knew that he would never have the guts. Edward intimidated Todd, in the way only an alpha dog could. Her father walked over to stand next to Lucy, but all she wanted him to do was go away.

"I'm here. I'm your dad, and you can't change that."

"I guess," she said.

"What's your play?"

"No idea."

Edward was ecstatic listening to her speak with someone he couldn't see. Lucy's eyes darted around the roof, searching for a weapon. Everything that seemed a possibility; old pipe, cement blocks, were all too far away. Edward was walking toward her.

"Maybe this will finally get things into that head of yours. We are on an open roof, yet I have no fear of an aircraft seeing what I do up here. Why do you think that is?"

"I don't know," she said.

Keep him talking.

"Because, nothing ever flies over this building. Never. Nothing happens that I don't want, do you understand?"

"Whatever you say."

That cinder block is too far, you'll never make it.

As if reading her mind, Edward said, "Don't bother," and reached into his pocket. He brought the small black remote control that would shock the life from her. He took a few more steps toward her, blocking the path to the cinder block even if she had wanted to take the chance.

Somehow, she had forgotten the collar. It had never been removed from her neck but also had never been used as a threat in all the time she was locked in the cage. It may as well have been a part of her own flesh.

"You are still hoping, aren't you?"

"For what?" Lucy asked.

"A way out, of course."

"I can't imagine I'll find one."

"No, I can't imagine you will either," Edward said, now a single foot away from Lucy. She looked over at her father. He had a proud look on his face that he had never shown her before. His eyes were telling her that it was okay, there was nothing she could do. He forgave her for letting herself down.

Todd was over by the dead woman, and though Lucy couldn't see for sure, she thought he was groping her. He was a pig, plain and simple. It was good that she let him die, and she would do it again now if she could. He looked up from the corpse and frowned.

All three men were looking at her, and she felt overwhelmed with hatred for the lot of them. Each had destroyed a piece of her, and each deserved their slow deaths. They didn't deserve to ride shotgun in Lucy's mind. That simply wasn't fair.

Edward. He was so pretty. Lucy grinned at him and this made his own smile fade. For a split second, he was taken aback; scared. She bent quickly down and swiped her hand across the roof, snagging a small, infant sized bone, cracked into a vicious point by careless feet. Edward didn't have the chance to react before Lucy was back up, shoving the hollow bone into his stomach.

His blood was warm as it gushed out onto her hand, the bone snagged on something inside of him as she pulled it out again. She felt the electricity enter her neck as she swiftly stabbed the baby's bone into Edward's neck, leaving it there.

She shook, while bile frothed from her mouth in an arc. Edward held his neck with one hand, clutching the control button with the other. He never would release it, and Lucy knew that. It was either just her or both of them. It was never going to be Edward alone. Life would never be that kind.

Heat spread through her fingertips, blackening them as she wrapped her arms around his body and pushed the two of them to the edge of the roof. She was now pulsing electricity into his body as well, but Edward refused to relent. Even as they tumbled over the edge, he kept his finger on the button.

The wind again.

As their bodies separated, Lucy felt an immense wind blowing from her back. Her matted hair looked like tentacles in the blue sky. She was falling so slowly; the edge of the roof moving away in a trickle of time. She looked at Edward. She was sure that his mouth was in a scream, but she didn't hear anything. Blood streamed from his mouth, elongating yet motionless as he dropped.

Still, the roof was in sight, and as she continued to fall, she saw the silhouettes of her father and Todd against the sun. Just as her moment was at hand, so too, were theirs. She hoped they were frightened.

She thought back to the punk kid from the popcorn shop. How would he act when he got older? Do people ever really change? She thought of Cassidy, always studying in the corner, and she regretted not finishing college for the forty-thousandth time.

I guess now is the time to let that go.
You are almost done.
Just a little bit further.
This pain is noth...

Friday, October 26, 2012

The Daily A

Woman falls to Death, Suicide

A local business owner fell from the Baxter building late Thursday afternoon. The name of the victim has not been released but authorities have stated that suicide was almost certain.

Multiple eyewitness reports stated that there was a second body on the scene but that has been confirmed false.

"We aren't releasing the name at this time but we have one victim, female. It appears that she jumped from the roof. There is no reason to suspect anything else at this time," said Detective Henderson with the local PD.

Crews had the area cleaned up just as the sun went down and traffic was only hampered for a short time.

Re foll im

The tha rea the beh ura exp in i its beh

227

I would like to take this time to acknowledge a few people who have helped me on this journey.

Jennifer Chang who designed the cover for *Strawberries* and was a great help for this book too.

Linda Autrey, because even though she got overwhelmed with life, she was a huge help and inspiration to me.

All of the people that were so generous during my Indie Go-Go campaign. I have amazing friends and family that are super supportive.

And last, but certainly not even close to least, my wife – **Lindsay Jones**. She puts up with so much bullshit while I am going through this process, fully knowing that it will never end. I love you!

Other books by the Author
Strawberries

Visit the author's website at:
http://www.CaseyBartsch.com/

Visit the author's blog devoted to all things horror:
http://www.FullBlownPanicAttack.com/

Sign up for the newsletter at either of those sites to get all the latest info on new books and other fun stuff. Don't worry, I won't spam your box until in explodes or anything.

Thanks to everyone who have given my book a chance! You are all the shit.

ABOUT THE AUTHOR

Casey Bartsch lives in a tiny Texas town called Belton. He has yet to meet any of his neighbors, or travel farther than the grocery store. He doesn't eat healthy foods, and is therefore a bit rotund. His girlfriend loves him anyway, and that works out well.

Casey often struggles to find the time to write. That is a lie. The time is plentiful. He just has a hard time choosing to write when other, less mentally taxing activities are available. He feels a great deal of regret each time he makes this wrong choice.

Casey spends an obscene amount of time trying to figure out why people do what they do, why he does what he does, and how long it might take before the world implodes in on itself and leaves him stranded on a small rock floating through the emptiness of space.

Lightning Source UK Ltd.
Milton Keynes UK
UKHW041327201020
371876UK00004B/748